THE ILLUMINATION
A NOVEL OF THE GREAT WAR

K.J. WETHERHOLT

Excerpts from The Ballad of the White Horse by G.K. Chesterton, "Aftermath" by Siegfried Sassoon, *An Choimiede Dhiaga* (with translation), WWI trench newspaper and song excerpts not demonstrably in the public domain are used with permission.

Cover and Author Photos by Pamela I. Theodotou (www.theodotou.com)

A Humanitas Media Print Publishing Edition.   _

For any information or permission to reproduce selections from this book, please send all correspondence via email to: editor@humanitasmedia.com.

http://www.humanitasmedia.com

ISBN: 978-0-9912917-5-5 (Third Edition)

Library of Congress Cataloging-in-Publication Data Wetherholt, K.J. (Kristin Jan), 1972 –

The Illumination: A Novel of the Great War

1. World War, 1914 – 1918. I. Title

To my great-grandfather...and to the man from the Grail dream.

Do you remember when we went
Under a dragon moon,
And 'mid volcanic tints of night
Walked where they fought the unknown fight
And saw black trees on the battle-height,
Black thorn on Ethandune?
And I thought, "I will go with you,
As man with God has gone,
And wander with a wandering star,
The wandering heart of things that are,
The fiery cross of love and war
That like yourself, goes on."

-- The Ballad of the White Horse, G.K. Chesterton (1917)

PROLOGUE

He could hear her calling to him. The soft strength of her voice carried on the winds which, for the last several days, had battered the Pyrenees, their steep black cliffs dropping sharply to the hills and forests of the valley below as thunderheads passed above, threatening to unleash an unforgiving torrent.

His pen moved across the page, scratching against parchment. The only light which was visible was that of a candle resting beside him, illuminating only a portion of his face and his dazed, almost haunted expression, as though he were in another world.

He continued, bent over his desk, barely hearing the movement of the branches and the rustling of leaves, their lifeless shells moving across the nearly frozen ground, the oncoming maelstrom soon to follow. Outside the wind had continued its otherworldly sound, almost like those of whispers, fading in and out of the storm.

Beside him was the ragged black-and-white photograph, the vision of her as he had remembered her, her long hair falling in waves across her shoulders. She was dressed unusually for a woman, in a man's white shirt, army breeches and brown jacket with its RAMC patch on the shoulder. She leaned casually against a British ambulance from the Great War, smiling knowingly into the camera.

The man paused, closing his eyes as he turned from the manuscript, the image of her remaining in the blackness, his expression filled with pain as he whispered harshly into the room. "Maeve…"

The young Englishman sat silently in the club dining room, which on any weekday was filled wall-to-wall with notable and aristocratic men who sat drinking brandy and continuing the same staid conversations over their cigars, many of them foregoing their afternoon meal for another drink. He watched these men silently, sitting in their dark leather chairs at tables fashioned out of teak and dark polished hardwood, each in throes of haughty laughter, rustling their newspapers and striking matches and flint to light up as they sucked the fragrant smoke of expensive tobacco through pursed lips.

He had waited alone, arriving as early as he did to make sure he was there when his father-in-law arrived, in the process, out of deference, waving away a servant who came by to ask him if he wanted a drink. Within moments of one o'clock, the distinguished older gentleman whom he had been waiting for approached, nodding a greeting to a few fellow members before heading over to his son-in-law's table. Locke stood, offering his hand to shake. Forsythe was an impressive gentleman, tall and handsome with penetrating blue eyes, and even in his sixties, his demeanor seemed to be the simple result of living an impeccable and aristocratically prescribed life. The silver-haired older gentleman smiled, taking the younger man's hand coolly as he sat down, indicating that Locke should do the same. Forsythe took an antique silver cigarette case from his jacket pocket, waiting only a few moments before an attendant stepped forward, instantly striking a match and waiting just until after his cigarette was lit before stepping out of sight. The older man took a short drag and looked down, glancing absently toward an open parcel which Locke had placed on the table.

"How is my daughter, Peter—keeping you on your toes?"

"She's doing well, sir."

"And the office? Is Jane surviving without me to run her through her paces?"

The younger man nodded, noting the reference to the older man's former secretary. She, as had the others before her, worked with several generations of Forsythes in the publishing house Harrold Forsythe's great-grandfather had established, as with most men of his station, as more of a hobby than as an occupation. Such gentlemen were then as they were now, every morning and afternoon sitting amidst the rarefied air of fellow aristocrats who continued to watch the outside from a distance, as though refusing to offer recognition would keep the world as it had become from their hallowed halls. Forsythe remembered well the looks on younger men's faces when introduced into the reality of this immutable world of stodgy old relics, forced to listen to the endless reminiscences of adventures in the colonies or some beloved horse or hound whose companionship rivaled that of one of their own wives. It was a tradition carried out from time immemorial, Forsythe thought silently, as his son-in-law would one day learn. The passing of a privileged torch from one generation to the next, assuring a sense of continuity to those who seemed to cling to it the most.

Forsythe nodded to the parcel Locke had brought with him, studying the expression on the younger man's face. "You've forgotten we fine you a bottle of port if one of us catches you working," he said evenly. "It keeps young men from working too hard to impress the rest of us with their ambition."

"It came into the office over the weekend. Jane thought you had better have a look."

Forsythe frowned slightly, picking up the package to get a closer look. It had been some time since he had bothered to read any manuscript which had passed through the doors of the house which bore his name, most knowing even before his retirement that he rarely took the time to walk into the office much less read what they were about to publish. Instead he waited until those chosen works came to him bound in rich leather with gold leaf, his family name emblazoned in small letters on the foot of the book's spine. His nonchalance was something Jane knew well, for she was the one who continued to send the result of the editors' labors. But now he paused, seeing the handwriting on the brown parcel paper holding yellowed pages, the strong, even cursive bearing a name he hadn't seen for some time.

Locke watched, waiting for several more moments as he suddenly found himself trying to read the older man's expression. Whatever gulf had already existed between them seemed now to widen even further. For a moment the sounds of the dining room had disappeared. All either man heard was the draft moving through the dining room as distant sounds seemed to rise from some dormant part of the older man's memory. The rest remained an uneasy silence.

Locke addressed him quietly. "You knew him? The man whom this is from?"

Forsythe paused for several moments. "He was someone I knew years ago—during the war."

A waiter approached, ready to take their order. Locke shook his head slightly, taking control long enough to send the waiter away, in whatever small way he could protect the older man from disruption, even as he continued to sink further into an ominous and distant fog. His reaction to the remembrance of war did not come as a surprise. Men who had fought on the varying fronts had all been the same in their reaction. Their faces became drawn, their eyes revealing a strange hollow pain, causing them to turn away with a sullen frown, as though no one would understand if they were to describe what they were feeling. He saw the same expression now in his father-in-law's countenance as Forsythe sat in his sudden, uninterrupted silence, steeling himself against whatever emotions had begun to stir as he stared absently out into space, the present moment having all but disappeared.

Forsythe sat in a worn leather chair in the library of his house in Kensington. Books he had published prior to his retirement and others which had been important to him over the years surrounded him on shelves which covered every available inch of space. The room was silent, the only sound that of the flames crackling against the dryness of the wood in the old stone fireplace, blackened from years of use. On the walls of the room were numerous photographs, of family, of his wife, of parents, relatives and friends long deceased.

Forsythe raised his head, after several hours, now staring up at a photograph of two haggard men standing beside an army lorry on a dusty road, their arms around each other's shoulders. He saw his own countenance, unmarred by age, the handsome, smooth features broadened into a smile. The years had been as unforgiving as he had expected them to be. His once light brown hair was now silver, his long, athletic frame thin and gnarled by the years since the war, war injuries having rendered him a semi-invalid depending on the weather and the roughshod way he treated himself, refusing to believe he was as old as he was. His eyes were the only thing that remained familiar, the blue irises faded in the photograph until almost appearing translucent, his expression one of an aristocratic sense of entitlement the Irishman in the photograph had always hated in him and had taken every opportunity to chide.

He remembered coming to the front from Nairobi in 1918, his skin tanned and leathery, his hair bleached by the sun, dressed in gear appropriate for a safari rather than overcast skies, chilled, damp air and several inches of mud. Burke had met him, laughing drunkenly and wondering what the hell had wandered in from the wilds, as though the Englishman were someone more prepared to play cricket than slog through mud to meet soldiers dying by the thousands in the field. And so he had been then, before experiencing the war as during those last weeks, and before the events that would bring him home.

Burke, too, was as he remembered, the rugged Celt

existing instead in that famous embittered, self-imposed silence, seeing the chaos around him and reveling in it as though it would give him the opportunity to forget anything that had come before. And beside Burke stood the striking young woman in a man's shirt and British military breeches, long, dark blonde hair falling as a mane against her back. Her manner reflected a strange combination of refinement and poetry, her strangely patrician countenance contradicted by the intensity and passion in her penetrating gray eyes. Behind her in the background was a company of soldiers moving with their packs hung heavily over their shoulders, most of them young men, many not even twenty years old. Even in the photograph he could see the looks on their faces marked the fear of what loomed before them, each step moving them closer to a destination away from the safety of the cafes and brothels of Paris.

Several moments later, Forsythe turned, picking up the manuscript gently. His hand shook despite himself as he laid his palm flat against the coarseness of the paper, the handwriting covering the page in a hard, masculine cursive. Even before he read the words, he could hear the gravel tones of Burke's voice, the strange half-brogue calling out to him from the blackness. He closed his eyes, feeling the sudden, almost visceral resurrection of the past, sensations he once felt now again moving through him—the cold dampness of the base near Amiens, the chill in the air, the wind howling, and the sweet, dank oak taste of stale whisky. And along with it came a faded image of a man and woman dancing before a fire as he watched from a distance, the deep stroke of her voice alone haunting him. They had been mirror images of each other, he remembered, she and Burke. The way they had spoken, their expressions, even the movement of their bodies as they had danced.

Harrold stared down at the page. For years since his return from the war he had convinced himself that none of those memories had existed, except in some part of his mind which he had prayed would become impenetrable over the years. But now, holding the Irishman's words in his hands, he knew he would never be able to escape those few months he had consigned to the most remote and unreachable part of his mind. The war had left an immutable void within him, and not even the imposed normalcy of his life when he returned home had restored it. He had not wanted to think of the man and woman who had been his friends, or what had happened to each of them in those weeks just before Armistice. Men who should have been enemies in another part of the world for a brief moment had become friends, seeing one another as human, knowing that perhaps moments later one or more of them would stare headlong into death. And that knowledge alone made each of them realize that no matter what happened in the war or when it was finally over, when the world would one day attempt to rebuild what had been lost, nothing would ever be the same.

PART ONE

THE WESTERN FRONT, FRANCE 1918

"The sight of them haunts us, taut with supreme effort,
a fearful grin stretches on dead men's dirty faces…
through the mist and drizzle, the rattle of death still
sounds."

-- La Musette (1916)

It was a weekend when the Irishman arrived back in Paris, seeing from the window of the military transport the multitudes of people milling around the street. Men and women stood warming their hands, watching as Allied soldiers and others who had been stationed from Arras to the Argonne began climbing out of transports which had arrived in the city over the last hour, stopping at various points from the east near Montmartre toward the tenth arrondissement. Men of every age now on leave emerged soiled and weary, slinging heavy packs over their shoulders, their breath visible in the morning air as one or another looked for a familiar face in the crowd, the only thing on his mind being a hot meal, a bath, and a good shot of whisky.

Burke climbed down with them, standing on the street watching the soldiers disperse, pausing just long enough to light the cigarette in his hand. His gray-green eyes burned from lack of sleep and his clothing was covered with bloodstains and mud. Like others in uniform, it had been perhaps a week since he had been able to bathe, even longer since he had been able to sleep more than a few hours at a time, sometimes less depending on how active the fighting had been during his time on the line. He knew no one would here be waiting for him, having made a point not to know anyone well enough to warrant any kind of impassioned homecoming. Instead he turned, walking down toward his hotel several blocks from the station, leaving the transport and the multitudes of soldiers behind.

The city was as he remembered it as he continued walking, feeling the air against his skin. The atmosphere was close and ancient, as though having lingered from previous centuries, breeding a kind of hard and enigmatic impenetrability among its inhabitants, as though even some part of their souls had been extracted from the centuries' old stone and mortar. It was this impenetrability that had caused Paris to remain as normal as could have been expected during the past three years of war, her citizens having gone on with their lives almost out of spite, even while the distant thunder of long range artillery fire rumbled from the nearest segment of the front. The Kaiserschlacht had made the city the primary target as the enemy troops entrenched only miles away, having managed at varying points to hold Soissons and Chateau-Theirry in their attempt to move toward the capital. Weeks before, shells from German "Paris Guns" had managed to enter the city from the Laon Corner seventy-five miles away, leveling the church of Saint-Gervais across from the Hôtel de Ville, leaving eighty-eight dead and more wounded when a stone pillar crumbled from the blast. It was the closest the city had come to understanding the carnage which had been commonplace only miles away, or in cities and villages closer to the front lines where Allied forces had been encamped. There what was once pristine grassland and forest before the war had become a wasteland, entire villages demolished, ancient churches razed to the ground in the endless bombardment, fire leaving skeletons of stone to remind the world of what had once existed.

Burke continued walking, the sounds of battle echoing from miles away. The sound had become so familiar that it barely seemed to register in his mind, having heard it since he had been stationed near Amiens. Like the soldiers who had come back to the city on leave, all he wanted was to drop off his gear and have a drink after filing his latest story—already censored by Allied command—with the wire service. For weeks he had experienced the stale and sullied air of the front, the sour winds filled with remnants of tear and poison gas coming from fields of battle. And he had only a day to rid these things from his mind, if even for a moment, before he returned, battle-wearied and hungover, heading with the soldiers back to the line.

Moments later, he heard his name being called. He turned to find two soldiers coming toward him. Like him, they were still dressed in khaki combat gear, barda and muddied boots, their rifles slung over their shoulders when they should have been freshly dressed and packed for leave. They were Australians whom he had known from the front lines, covering the front to the north of Reims with their detachment of the ANZAC which had been fighting with their British counterparts among the Third and Fourth Armies of the British Expeditionary Force.

"Burke, you bloody bastard—"

One of them grinned and came up shaking his hand.

"Christ—look a little worse for wear, don't you, mate?"

Burke shook the Aussie's hand and smiled, as he offered Burke a rusted flask. He took a swig and handed it back, frowning. The Aussie, not looking like he had had a fresh shave in days laughed, seeing the Celt's face. "It's bourbon from the Yanks." He then nodded absently toward the east, as though indicating the front. "We've got one of your replacements coming in. They're stationing him with you near Amiens. Some ponce reporting for the wire service."

Burke frowned, shifting his weight in irritation. The bloke who hadn't yet spoken then piped up as he slapped Burke on the shoulder, as though to sink the dagger more deeply. "Too bad, mate. A limey of all things— out of Nairobi. Spiffed like he just got in from playing cricket. Don't know what he would have had to report on except some pommy bastard getting the clap at Muthaiga." The Australian coughed, laughing as he lit a cigarette. "I'd like to see him downing hard tack knee-deep in the mud."

"What's his name?"

"Harrold Forsythe. He's waiting for you at the Pommes Bleues. You can't miss him…looks like he just got back from safari."

The other Aussie grinned at the thought. "Bloody-well give him a proper bollicking. The knob will need it rough for practice before things go pear-shaped on the line."

The other one started heading away, casting another gratified comment in the Irishman's direction. "No nicer bloke to do the job."

Several freshly dressed soldiers approached the small bar known in infamy as the Pommes Bleues on the corner of the Rue Charlotte on the edge of Paris, accompanied by a few of the many young women who regularly availed themselves to soldiers, offering perfunctory companionship while looking for a good time. The bar was loud even from the street, with laughter and music coming from the closed doorway. It was one of the few establishments that carried Scotch, Irish whiskey and beer acquired on the black market, thereby attracting British, ANZAC, Canadians and Americans who wanted to be reminded of being back home. Inside, flags from the various member nations of the Allied forces hung on the darkened panel walls, along with other artifacts brought back from the front. Anonymous black-and-white photographs hung on the smooth paneled hardwood, many of them framed, others torn and covered with nondescript stains, as though they had been hidden in the pockets of soldiers in the field. Some of the photographs were of girlfriends, others of wives and children, but many of them were of soldiers in the camps from Belgium to the

Argonne, arms over each other's shoulders in a palpable camaraderie as they smiled into the camera.

Burke sauntered over to the bar, ordering a bottle of whiskey. Beside him soldiers and reporters on weekend leave sat with prostitutes on their laps, all of them carrying on as the cacophony of drunken laughter and singing filled the air. *"Another little drink, another little drink, oh another little drink wouldn't do us any harm…"*

The barman peered at the Irishman curiously, as though not sure whether or not to give him another drink. The surly Celt was older than many of the soldiers, ruggedly solid, and if provoked, itching for a fight. Like other men who had been exposed to war for far too long, he had the wry and wearied indifference of an embittered wanderer who had isolated himself, convinced it was far easier to comment on the nature of humanity without knowing anyone all too well.

Burke glared at the bartender sharply. "Whisky."

The bartender got out a glass and began to pour a Dewar's. Burke shook his head, his tone changing, his voice dropping to a caustic growl. "No—the bottle."

The bartender handed the bottle over without argument and watched as Burke moved with it and the glass to his lone table in the back corner of the bar away from the crowd. He slumped into the chair and poured roughly a triple shot, swigging it immediately as he surveyed the commotion around him. Drunken men and women were caught in the throes of varying forms of escapism, the same mix of characters who had frequented the well-known establishment over the last years, men who didn't give a damn about anyone or anything and would leave someone in need of solitude well enough alone.

It wasn't long before Burke felt someone's eyes on him. He looked across the floor, noticing a man staring at him from a table a few feet away. He was a handsome man, rugged, an aristocrat from the look and cut of his togs. Burke poured another shot and spoke loudly enough for the man to hear, calling across the short distance between them.

"You look like you just got in from a bloody cricket match."

The Englishman looked at Burke as though irritated, hearing the rough brogue and the man, equally rough, to whom it was attached. "That's the bottle of Scotch. Looks like you're set on finishing it."

Burke studied him for a moment, then turned back toward the bar, calling behind him to the barman who moved quickly, placing a tumbler on the bar before the Irishman had to ask a second time. The Englishman watched as Burke stood, taking the glass and placing it and the half-finished bottle on the Englishman's table and poured Scotch into both glasses.

"What do they have you covering?"

The Englishman noticed that it wasn't really a question. "The line near Amiens. How did you know?"

Burke bowed his head, a wry smirk growing across this mouth. "You're not wearing a uniform. And you're not a civilian." He paused, looking the man in front of him over.

The Englishman sat back in the chair. "I suppose you're covering some part of this skirmish."

Burke grunted in derision he looked down and noted a ring on the Englishman's finger. "Tell me, are you prepared to leave your wife a widow?"

The Englishman bristled. "God, man—what kind of question is that?"

"A good one for a man who has never set foot in the trenches." Burke paused again, seeing his drinking companion suitably racked off as he lit a cigarette.

"As it happens, my wife is about to have our second child," Harrold said with a certain degree of irritation. "The War Office saw fit to have me play war hero closer to home."

Burke gave the Englishman a piercing look, as though cutting past the bullshit. "You won't be going home anytime soon. And you won't remember you have a wife and child."

A sudden crash interrupted them. Two servicemen were fighting over a belle de jour who stood at the bar, now turning her attention to someone else who might be willing to buy her a drink. Harrold stared at her, as did the rest of the bar before turning back to their previous conversations.

Burke chuckled quietly under his breath, his deep voice again sounding off as though half to himself, half to the rightly-described pommy bastard before him. "War makes whores of us all."

∞

The army transport drove slowly onto the camp near the Somme River south of Albert, behind it a large supply lorry from the British Red Cross. From the back, Harrold stared outside watching the soldiers, most of them young men, several years younger than he would have expected, the lot of them, their number several hundred or more, congregating into their companies after several days in the rear, preparing for the next German offensive.

The trip from Paris had been long, the few correspondents having been given leave to cover the line were all veterans except for Harrold, men who had seemed to regard his presence with a certain degree of irritation. They had met at the Press Office—a bare, bustling room filled with desks, where censors were going over each dispatch, finalizing each report before it was considered acceptable for the wire. They had been there only moments, Burke having received their orders, ones he had already anticipated and confirmed, that the Englishman was to be assigned with him to cover the line near Amiens. With their introduction, both men had bristled at the idea, but had gone without word to the train taking them to the

last stop for munitions, horses, supplies, and soldiers on the
Allied rail line from Paris before reaching the front, and
where they, along with several other journalists back from
leave would catch a motor transport to the line.

Several hours later, the lorry stopped in front of a
section of barracks, soldiers unloading gear from the back.
Both Burke and Harrold continued to be hungover as they
climbed down from the tailgate, each of them pulling out
their blankets and packs, having sustained whatever marked
antagonism from the night before during those hours with
silence, each of them feeling the distinct and mordant effects
of the last few rounds of Scotch. Burke turned, catching
Harrold's attention as he nodded to a distant section of the
camp.

"We're over there. That section of barracks.
They've been billeting correspondents together here since
GHQ first allowed us on the front. Then there were only
five of us who could get accredited to cover the line. Now
there are more than that, but the rules haven't changed. No
names of soldiers, companies, or locations." Burke took a
drag on his cigarette, nodding toward the far end of the
camp where they were headed. "You'll take direction from
the resident press officer. And he gets information we're
allowed to print from the I.O...." He paused to make sure
Harrold was keeping up, "the intelligence officer. That
should tell you how much truth there is in the reports."

"And I'd heard things had changed since Kitchener
was laid six feet under."

The Englishman had meant the comment to be
ironic, knowing Kitchener to be the one man universally
reviled—even in memory—by veteran correspondents for
the stranglehold he had once placed on the press, but he
soon realized that any such statement, ironic or otherwise,
would most likely fall on deaf, if not hostile ears.
Kitchener's tactics and attitude toward the press had been
mercenary, and men like Perceval Phillips, William Beach
Thomas, Philip Gibbs, Herbert Russell, and Perry

Robinson had been allowed limited access to the line since the War Office had first allowed the presence of accredited correspondents. They were subject to military law, forced to comply with the direct orders of their commanding officers, which were more often than not a ranking field censor. Any material which was even remotely useable by the enemy, directly or indirectly, was promptly censored, and if allowed to go to press would cause both the journalist and his censor to be brought up on charges. It was what Kitchener, head of the War Office until his death in 1916, had in mind when first allowing correspondents on the front, before it was discovered that reporters were an easy means of putting a victorious face on an otherwise bloody and disheartening war.

Harrold watched as Burke walked ahead without comment. Harrold slung his pack over his shoulder, feeling the restriction of the weight he was being forced to carry. He had changed into the same uniform Burke also wore—the worn khakis of a BEF infantryman which on the Irishman seemed to cling like a second skin to his powerful frame. Harrold noticed Burke also wore the harp and crown badge which belonged to the Second Royal Irish Regiment of the Sixteenth Irish Division, whom Burke had covered off and on since its inception and its deployment to Le Havre, following Parliament's acceptance of the idea of an all- Nationalist Volunteer Irish Division in 1914. Like its predecessor, the Tenth, which had been made up of both Catholics and Protestants from the north and south of Ireland, and had since been shuttled throughout the varying armies from their deployment to Salonika onto the Eastern Front and later to Palestine, the Sixteenth had also been constantly under threat that their numbers would be spread throughout the British Expeditionary Force. Tensions had been pronounced among British command since the Easter Uprising in Ireland in 1916, fearing that the Nationalist forces would soon revolt against their BEF officers—a revolt which never happened. Having fought alongside their

British counterparts, as well as other Colonial forces, considering the depth and resonance of shared experience among them, including the death of friends and others who had shared the same ground and miles of trenches on the front, any thought of rebellion in those moments would have marked a brutal and unforgivable disloyalty.

Regardless of his source of origin, Burke had since his first year on the front acquired a certain degree of infamy, having been assigned to cover the war throughout British positions along the front, for some reason not having been held under the same restrictions as other journalists. Harrold, like others who had instantly recognized the name if not the man himself, had wondered what it was about Burke that had intimidated his commanding officers, enough for him to be comparatively unencumbered by the same rules forced upon other press. Having met him, he now understood. The man had a brutal discernment that seemed to create an instant sense of defensiveness among anyone with something to hide. From having read the reports which Burke had written, both for the public and for the trench papers in the field, the latter of which had become infamous among the enlisted, it had become clear that his loyalties were squarely with fellow soldiers, especially when faced with the "glory" other journos—who had never reached the front lines— had sold to the public, and distinctly under orders. Even if it were for papers written and distributed only among them, the Irishman had depicted the true nature of war about which the realities of engagement might never otherwise be known. And while the War Office attempted to use him for their purposes, Burke would find a way to use them for his, for those men whom he considered his natural brethren, giving them some sense that their experiences were not forgotten.

The Western Front had always been a world with which Harrold was unfamiliar, this world of hardcore colonial divisions, each to him seeming rougher and more jaded than the next, and he knew he had only scratched the

surface during the few hours he had spent ensconced among
Allied forces. Although he now wore the same BEF
uniform as the Irishman, he found himself feeling
claustrophobic, and it was as much from the cold, heavy
dampness in the air as it was from the clothes on his back. It
was an unfamiliar sensation, having previously been in the
open air, feeling the dusty earth, dry and cracked, the heat
unbearable in the day and the cold descending without
warning at night. He had worn the standard togs familiar
among his East African regiment— a wide-brimmed hat, an
open-necked bush shirt and shorts, and whatever rifles they
had acquired from their own gun cases. The war had been
as much an excitement as a concern among those living
both within and around Nairobi, urgent meetings having
been called by the local aristocracy for the sole purpose of
throwing themselves into whatever skirmish might avail
itself. Instantly, those with connections sent request to
British command for more munitions than there were men,
other weapons having been amassed from British shipments
into Mombasa or from Somalis who had dealt in massive
amounts of useable weaponry following the Boer War. The
Colonials had been anxious to join newly and often
haphazardly-designated volunteer regiments, rallied on by
local aristocrats like Lord Delamere, for whom, like many
other similarly constituted sportsmen, war was akin to going
on a hunting expedition. At first there had been little to do
but drink whisky, amass in camps from Utegi to Lake
Natron and talk about the movements of von Lettow-
Vorbeck, the German officer in command of the
Schutztruppe who had once been welcomed among them at
various colonial watering holes. Harrold had been on a
several-year stint in Nairobi when the war had begun, and
having already sent his wife home to London, in a drunken
bout of nationalism offered his services to the British Army
while losing at cards. His reports had been ones showing
more men falling victim to malaria, syphilis and black-water
fever than to active engagement. But when engagement

with German forces did occur in short bursts entailing often deadly skirmishes, it was almost impossible to receive accurate reports until several days later, with territories covering an area of thousands of square miles.

The front as experienced in the German and British East African colonies was a different theater of war, and never had he realized the extent to which that was truer than after arriving in Paris. The few weeks since he had left Nairobi had been filled with reports which were sometimes over a week old and heavily censored, news having traveled slowly from the varying fields of battle, the war having infiltrated the colonial strongholds of three different continents. Burke seemed to know all too innately how the similarity of the stories among men caused the Colonial forces to continue to band together through the hard merits of shared experience. And just coming from Nairobi, it would only be natural Harrold had faced the kind of editorial commentary regarding the rarefied bloke who had just arrived to watch the fight, unproven in their neck of the woods. Their derision would further be leveled upon anyone who believed war was won through sheer force of character than the total war existing in reality on the fields, having heard about upper crust colonials of East Africa, and with him now here, expecting him to have brought with him one of the native askaris as an attaché, dutifully toting one of the infamous elephant guns they had heard so much about.

In the meantime, Harrold was struggling under the weight of his pack, uncomfortably shouldering his load as he had seen the infantry do with relative ease. The pack was heavy, though significantly smaller than the packs supported by barda the infantry were forced to carry which were sometimes up to seventy or eighty pounds depending upon the time of year. With the cold mornings filled with fog and the seeming unending rain, they continued to carry their long coats and blankets, which added the additional weight. He grunted derisively to himself, thinking that one thing would have been true—had he been in the colonies, the native element would have served the press corps, carrying whatever supplies they needed. But then it shouldn't have been much different, or so he would have surmised, having heard that even correspondents on the western front had once been allowed at least a single servant or attaché, and wondered why such still wasn't the case.

Burke finished his cigarette and lit another as they began walking along the dirt road toward a far section of barracks, along the way noting the indentations in the soil carved out by whippet tanks that had recently been introduced to the front. Burke called out behind him. "It hasn't rained for the last few days, so you won't have to worry about the mud—you'll get used to that soon enough." He then paused, glancing behind him. "But watch out for the horseshit. The cavalry lines are downwind from the barracks."

Harrold looked down, seeing amidst the dirt piles of manure, one of the officers' cobs from the cavalry snorting nearby, several others being led through the camp to prepare for transport. "Christ…"

Burke laughed, amused by Forsythe's irritation enough to let further commentary go until they reached their current destination. Lines of tents and several bivouacs from soldiers waiting for their orders reached far across the field, several of them part of the Third and Fourth Army command, men sitting before small fires, eating, or writing letters home. As they walked past, the sight of several young soldiers hauling the multitudes of lifeless bodies, most of them stuffed into makeshift bags and into lorries for burial stopped him in his tracks. Harrold stared at them in silence, then moved forward, noting that Burke was already far ahead of him and not looking back.

Within an hour of arriving, Harrold lay on the rough, stained cot in the small press barracks, having unpacked a letter which had been sent on to him at his hotel in Paris, and which he hadn't read since his arrival. Beside him was a photograph of his wife. He stared at it as though trying to re-familiarize himself with her features, though he knew it had not been even a day since he had last seen it. Burke watched from a couple of feet away. He could make out a darkly beautiful young woman standing in the thick of a well-kept English garden, which from the look of it could easily have been on the picturesque corner of any Englishman's country estate. Then, absently noticing the writing on the back, he was able to glean that the picture had indeed been taken in Devonshire, as Burke had expected. Burke glanced at Harrold, noting his strangely dispassionate manner, as though there were more than a physical distance between husband and wife. He smiled caustically to himself, deciding to abbreviate whatever stolid reverie in which the colonial had found himself and reached inside of his pack. Harrold, seeing his movement, glanced up, watching as Burke tossed a packet of cigarettes onto Harrold's chest, the suddenness of the action startling him. Burke then took out one of his own cigarettes, nodding to the pack he had just tossed to the man in the next cot.

"They're the best currency you've got. There's nothing a soldier wants more than a smoke, a drink, and some tart-up showering him with attention. You got one of them, and it'll make a difference between getting a story and leaving without one." Burke lit the cigarette in his hand, taking a drag before continuing. "You'll submit all communications to the field censors before sending them on the wire to the Press Office. From there your reports will be sent on to the wire service. You'll be tempted to tell the censors or the Press Office to go fuck themselves, but it's better to disseminate propaganda in your own words than see what they come up with. Considering a lot of the field censors are chaplains, you'd better be especially careful if you accidentally submit a letter you've written to your wife." He chuckled, seeing Harrold's expression. "The priests can handle whatever they hear, as they hear everything in confession. Church of England would rather hold court among the other officers in the rear over gins and tonic." He looked at Harrold. "Men of the cloth, whose role it is for the sake of God and country to lie to the public for the greater good."

Harrold frowned, irritated by both the commentary and the man who was leveling it as he tossed the packet of cigarettes onto his cot. "I should divest you, Burke, of the mistaken impression that I don't know what the bloody hell I'm doing."

"You're not at Muthaiga. You don't." The Englishman's jaw tightened. Burke smiled to himself. "Go to sleep. We've got an early start in the morning."

It was just before dawn, the first light not yet over the horizon as the camp began to awaken. Harrold emerged from the tent to find Burke waiting for him. The Englishman appeared as though he hadn't had even a moment of real sleep, his eyes bloodshot from tossing and turning on a cot which wasn't too different even from sleeping on the ground. He was clearly uncomfortable in BEF khakis and the heavy load of gear he hadn't had to carry in weeks, if at all, whether it had been on the East African front or on the boat which had brought him back to Europe.

Burke nodded toward one of several lorries waiting to take a company of soldiers and a small corps of reporters to the front, several sections having arrived from the same rail lines—stopping just outside of Amiens—that they had traveled the day before. Burke dropped the butt of his lit cigarette to the ground, stamping it out as he nodded toward the far section of the camp.

"Wait here. I'll see which transport we're supposed to take to the line."

Harrold frowned slightly, watching soldiers mustering several feet away. The soldiers themselves were as old as forty, cleanly shaven and after several days of endless drilling, square bashing and filling sandbags in the rear, ready out of sheer boredom to head back to the line. Despite the jokes that seemed to fly, and the anticipation of anything other than days of mindless activity overseen by officers who would never see the front line, their expressions, for the most part, were emotionless, as though preparing themselves out of necessity for what they knew they would find when they arrived back in the trenches.

He moved with the other journalists, while Burke motioned him toward one of several transports. The transports were stopped next to the surgical units of the camp, several medics standing silently, waiting for wounded coming in from the fighting near Albert, where Byng's forces had held ground despite massive pressure from the German Second Army. The camp was close enough to the front that it was the only place near the line where anything more than the most minor surgery could take place once leaving the varying aid posts and advanced dressing stations. This being one of the larger casualty clearing stations on the line, with its size having grown since the beginning of the war to house as many men as a stationary hospital. There was one medical officer and a nursing corps for each battalion, but none of the rules held with thousands of men coming into the camp on any given day, many of whom would later be sent to one of several base hospitals in the rear. Harrold observed the few nurses moving about, the few who were allowed there, for women were allowed to come no closer than a clearing station to battle, as much for their own safety as for being a distraction among the soldiers. He watched them darting among the infirmary tents, their long skirts and the red crosses emblazoned on their aprons. They were the only glimmer of civility that existed here, among the rough and desolate hoards of men, and he knew, too, that they were a sometimes painful reminder of what awaited them at home.

Harrold heard a noise, the sound of canvas as the flap on a nearby infirmary tent slipped down from where it had been awkwardly secured. Moments later, he saw a flash of blonde hair and the unusually striking young woman, in her early thirties, to whom it was attached. She moved quickly, grabbing the heavy canvas material acting as a barrier from the wind, the dust already being kicked up from the foot traffic of soldiers getting ready to move out. Several orderlies rushed to help her secure it, and despite English apparently being her first language, he listened to her as she cursed under her breath in an almost native French as the canvas fell once again. Harrold observed the standard khaki army clothing, and her jacket tied around her waist, on it the marks of an officer and the insignia of the Royal Army Medical Corps, with the words in Latin, *In Arduis Fidelis.*

He was immediately disarmed by the sight of her. Several wisps of her dark blonde hair had escaped and fallen in soft waves against her cheek, which she brushed away in annoyance. She continued turning her attention on the orderlies, directing them in a smooth, American English, exasperated from the irritation of being distracted as she looked once again inside the tent where a nurse was calling to her to come back in to surgery. He looked at her uniform more closely, seeing that it was indeed covered with spatters of dried blood, none of which she noticed, as though even to a woman it were a common sight. Harrold watched her with fascination, nothing else for the moment really seeming to matter but the distraction of a woman, not in nurse's uniform, near the line.

Burke watched Harrold stare for several moments, and then called out, heading toward the mud- covered lorry where soldiers had already begun to pile inside. Harrold took another last look around, The woman issued orders as she headed back into one of several surgical tents while leaving the rest of her orderly staff behind. He paused, staring for several more moments as, he noticed, the others around him did, before moving closer to the transport vehicle.

Harrold climbed inside and looked down the line at the sea of faces on either side of what was once a cattle lorry, several of the men talking, others sitting back, closing their eyes for the hour-long trip east to the active portion of the front. The journalists would stay for only a few days, much less than any of the soldiers, more often than not chaperoned while covering specific zones along the line and billeted away from engagement. The other journalists were already silent, knowing what awaited them, and knowing from experience that the soldiers, should they not level a few coarse words in their direction, would soon ignore them. He looked down the row of men. The soldiers held their rifles as though they were attached like another appendage, their bodies leaning against their packs, as the few journalists kept to themselves.

Harrold turned, curious as to Burke's reaction and discovered that he was instead already asleep, his head cocked to one side, his grizzled cheek unshaven. Burke's lower left sleeve caught his attention. On it were three narrow stripes, each one indicating having been wounded in battle, an odd distinction, he thought, for one who was known as a journalist. Harrold frowned slightly, then peered again at the soldiers, old and young alike, most of them jaded from their time on the line, staring out into space. It wasn't long before several others had ceased talking and, like Burke, had drifted into some deep slumber, despite the sharp smell of gasoline and the transport shaking violently as it lumbered forward. He did not yet know it was a defense mechanism as well as a necessity, for none of them would sleep well once they arrived on the line.

Since winter of 1918, and following the first years of war since its inception in 1914, Germany had moved forward with a dedicated shift in strategy. Already well-ensconced in the idea of the cult of the offensive and the notion of machine-like institutionalized war strategy which had marked German war philosophy since before the war began from the von Schlieffen Plan onward, with the Germans now fighting on only a single front from their own soil following the Treaty of Brest-Litovsk, military General Erich von Ludendorff had concentrated both efforts and men in his continued desire to push past the Somme. In March, Ludendorff had decentralized command across the western front, secretly deploying forty-seven special attack divisions and more than 6,000 guns across the German area of the line, shoring up twenty-eight trench divisions in what would serve the beginning assaults and which would become his strategic signature over the coming months, forcing an even more merciless war of attrition. Taking the same tactics which had been used on the eastern portion of the front in Riga, German and Austro-Hungarian troops were divided into two small groups:. the Angriffsdivisionen, which included the Stosstrupen, elite shock troops made up of young men who received the best weaponry and rations, their advance forces hitting during the darkness of morning with flamethrowers and short-range guns, followed successively by bursts of medium-range artillery. This would immediately be followed by the Stellungsdivisionen, a massive wave of regular infantry which would infiltrate and overrun the trenches, assaulting the Allied troops and continuing to push them back across the line. The initial wave of shock troops would blindside Allied forces by cutting diagonally behind their rear positions, the next waves of infantry were to defeat them while the shock troops continued to advance, once again striking without the customary frontal assault. No long-range artillery would be used to indicate their position, or their approach. It was a different plan used to cut to the core of the British sense of security. According to Ludendorff and the philosophy to which he had continued to subscribe, the amount of ground itself would not be so important as the surprise and brutalization which might cause the Allies to be intimidated enough to retreat. The closer the German troops were to Paris, the more likely they would be to eventually take it and cut the heart out of the Allied will to continue fighting.

With the newly-installed Bolshevik government securing their authority in Russia while losing 1.3 million square miles of territory in the interest of ceasing hostilities, the Germans and Austro-Hungarians welcomed the thought of further unmitigated conquest, including the attraction of re-drawing geographic boundaries in the West. What had once been a well-saturated stretch of ground would, over the next weeks, quickly become a veritable bloodbath coursing over miles of countryside of the Ardennes to Artois, Picardie, and Champagne. The offensive, known to the Germans as Operation Michael, had already succeeded in pushing the Allied forces past the Sambre, the Allied command scrambling to retrench, all the while leveling their own brutality at the German and Austro-Hungarian forces while in retreat, if only to buy themselves some time. Emergency meetings commenced among the Allied commanders, seeking to revise both strategy and to make changes to Allied command, disturbed by ground lost and the sheer numbers of casualties. With the Americans arriving in vast numbers, they were still being held in training camps until GHQ could determine the terms of their involvement. As Pershing had made clear, the United States was not about to blindly commit American soldiers to a war machine which had already proven both costly and unwieldy, and which had already led not only to millions of casualties, but also to numerous mutinies about which the Germans, as well as anyone outside Allied command, would know nothing about until after the war. The Allied forces and the Germans and Austro-Hungarians had fought a brutal, costly war for almost four years, and they were each scrambling to win before their total war of attrition left them both defeated in terms of men and firepower.

It was into this environment that Harrold now found himself, reporting, as did Burke, on the small portion of the reality which was a vastly different experience in the trenches than it was on paper, again, whether in the newspapers or in the reports sent back to operation commanders. It was something he had been told however dispassionately by Burke as a warning—one which would soon be borne out by the coming days. What he had read bore no resemblance to what he was witnessing, even upon approaching sections of the line not even considered zones of frontline combat. The vast machinery of war in terms of tanks, medium-range artillery, and sheer numbers of troops spread out across what he knew to be hundreds of miles of ground was instantly overwhelming. And it made the numbers of combatants, and their means of conducting the war half a world away seem deeply arcane in comparison. After the ensuing days, for the first time since his arrival, he would have the disquieting sense that those with whom he had served in colonial East Africa had not known what the British Empire had gotten herself into. The only ones who truly did were the men fighting. It was only then that he would understand what Burke and others who had seen the front lines meant, men who would continue to be castigated among more rarefied circles for the seeming unbelievability of even their written descriptions, which would continue years later, as though they were intended as some kind of unnecessary hyperbole meant to inflict pain or guilt on those who had not seen such sights for themselves. But for those who had experienced it, as Harrold would soon learn, it couldn't have been more the opposite. As he would soon find, no man would talk about his experiences if given the choice, if it weren't for some need to reach out to a different world when faced with endless moments of anticipation of combat on the front lines, if only to remember, for those few moments, a different world still indeed existed. What such men had described then, even in letters home if they weren't censored, if he weren't among others who had experienced what he had, would more than likely instead cause him to face being met with an uncomfortable silence among friends and family alike when finally returning home. Whatever outlets any man had in those moments on the line, from letters home to the necessary camaraderie among men, whatever forms such camaraderie took, were perhaps the very few things that would keep his soul alive. And without realizing it, being among such men, and seeing the effects of endless moments staring across the deep chasm which separated him from an impending onslaught, even as he watched the soldiers upon arriving on the line, some part of him could already sense that fate would see to it that he would become one of them.

Burke and Forsythe stood in the rear of one of the support lines to the immediate north of the Somme, having just come in from the reserve trench several hundred feet back. With the British Fifth Army now in ruins and its general having been dismissed, Haig had moved several divisions of ANZAC south to cover the area toward Bapaume along the ancient Roman road between Amiens and Albert until Sir Henry Rawlinson could take command of a newly designated Fourth Army. There they were hit by German bombardments but had managed to hold the line until the French could move north to meet their forces. The Germans had continued to attempt to drive a wedge between the Australian divisions and the French army, but had, to this point been unsuccessful, with the Australians and New Zealanders now holding close to fifteen miles of ground.

Burke had immediately been greeted by one of the several Australian officers of the Third Australian Division, having covered the line with their forces to the north some months before. Despite the seriousness of recent events on the line, as Harrold had heard even prior to reaching the front, it seemed the Australians and Irish got on rather famously, which became apparent when Burke was invited to the officer's quarters for a quick (and forbidden) drink before checking in with the division press officer. Harrold waited, watching soldiers milling around, waiting for news from the forward lines or packing their gear and loading requisitions for further movement. He could hear the sound of mortars in the distance, loud blasts muffled by the sand and dirt of the trench, as well as the laughter of several soldiers. He noticed that the noise again did not seem to bother any of these men, hardcore members of ANZAC infantry battalions who had been stationed in the east before being sent to the western portions of the front with the BEF, many of them having fought the Turks during a difficult and brutal engagement near Gallipoli. He listened to their commentary, the likes of which he could barely understand, their slang too rough and incomprehensible, he thought caustically, to be understood by much of anyone, even those below his own station, whom they were fighting alongside.

Within an hour, Burke checked in with a military liaison, and then the press officer, who handed Burke Harrold's papers. They were local registrations which, along with BEF accreditation, would allow the Englishman to move with him among the varying zones along the line. Burke barely spoke as he slapped his orders unceremoniously against Harrold's chest, staring toward one of the narrow traverses carved through the muddied ground which would head to one of the reserve lines. Motioning toward the traverse, they then began to move, accompanied by a section of infantry which was going in at the same time to replace other soldiers on the line ready for leave. They moved quietly through the mud, several jokes muttered wryly about the weather, as they continued their hour-long march to reach the spots they would hold for the coming hours. In the distance, they could hear the continued thunder of artillery reverberating in the close and claustrophobic atmosphere of the traverse, the inability to see over the walls of their passage causing Harrold to feel strangely disquieted, as though whatever might happen, he wouldn't be able to see coming. It was different enough from the nearly silent expansiveness he was used to in East Africa, that he could only bow his head in a confounded silence.

It was nearly dawn when they arrived, the sun having begun to rise over the horizon. Harrold peered forward, trying to see ahead of him. This was one of the more derelict areas of the line between Amiens and Albert, a wasteland hit by two different forces since the Germans first reached it in 1915. The trenches were filled with several inches of mud, duckboards covering the uneven ground, two long planks traversed by wooden slats. All around him the earthen walls had collapsed, having been re-buttressed by sandbags and scaffolding rising nearly seven feet high. Soldiers came and went, runners constantly taking communications among the sections, others bringing in wounded from the front lines. The stench was almost unbearable, that of dried blood, raw sewage, kerosene and rotting flesh. Rats ran through the trenches or lay dead, covered, like some of the men, with lice, emitting a stale, sour smell which after months on the line, as with numerous other irritating or disturbing nuances of frontline combat, in comparison with death had become a veritable afterthought. So far every infantryman he had seen had been covered head to foot in soiled gear and bloodstained clothing, whether the blood was their own or that of fellow soldiers

An ANZAC field officer barked to one of his sergeants as the two men watched, hearing the first mortars of morning hate exploding in the distance. Harrold paused, his jaw tensing, unable to see or hear anything but the distant sound of artillery fire, the ground shaking underneath their feet and beside them along the walls of the trench. Burke stared forward, watching the officers and their men as they prepared to run headlong into the front lines, gleaning information he could get just from the expressions on their faces.

"I take it we're not going with them."

Burke recognized Harrold's sarcasm, a tone he had known from experience to be the typical bravado of even an aristocrat's arrogant and well-bred sense of entitlement. He nodded toward the soldiers, now disappearing through the communications trench. He then looked at Harrold, his expression hard, as though in being on the line he had reverted to an even greater stoniness than he had shown in the rear. Burke then turned again, watching the last of the soldiers disappear, moving through the jagged formation of the communications trench. "We're just a distraction."

Harrold looked pointedly at Burke's stripes which he had seen the day before. He paused, his tone more than slightly ill-tempered. "From what I understand, you've been allowed by GHQ on the front line."

Burke continued staring forward, not wasting any time to end the conversation. "I've been here since the beginning," he said. "And they know I've got blood on my hands."

Harrold was about to respond when they both heard a cry, men shouting from several feet away. Stretcher bearers were weaving their way through the communications trench, bearing bodies from the front line as mortars continued exploding in the distance, shattering the air, the ground moaning and shaking beneath them. He could see that they were casualties from the first barrage of minenwerfer fire bombarding the line since morning hate.

Burke immediately cleared a path as the stretcher bearers called forward to alert the rear they were bringing another casualty to the dressing station. It was then that

Harrold saw what was being brought from the line. It was the body of an Australian soldier, his lower body nearly gone, flesh and bone exposed to the smoke-filled air, his upper body shuddering violently despite having been tied down on the stretcher. Harrold fixed on the boy's eyes, seeing that he was perhaps no more than twenty years old, though his body looked older, grizzled and leaned from previous engagement. As he was carried past, Harrold heard him muttering something over and over again in gibberish, an unintelligible series of words which after a moment Harrold realized was the Lord's Prayer.

The stretcher-bearers continued toward the communications trench and the rear of the line, their voices already hoarse from screaming into the day's maelstrom. Harrold then heard Burke mutter something under his breath to one of the officers, a lieutenant-colonel in command of the ANZAC battalion, and apparently a friend of Burke's, who had come in to observe the forward lines.

"He'll never make it past triage."

"It doesn't matter. He joined in Adelaide and survived the Turks before he came here. He's been the battalion's good luck charm. They're bloody-well going to try to save him."

Harrold turned back. The soldier's body heaved in sudden contortion as he continued gasping, his expression one of sheer horror from having seen his own body blown apart. As the stretcher-bearers waited for the communications trench to clear, Harrold watched the boy's eyes slowly begin to dull, his skin mottling as the blood stopped flowing, his expression falling as the boy took his last, labored breath. In his last moment, Harrold had seen the blistering from where the shrapnel had blasted through his body, leaving behind the carnage and the smell of burning, bloodied flesh. He could only have smelled his own body burning, waiting for the stretcher bearers to find him. Seeing the face of death, the acrid smell of smoke, remnants of gas, burning metal and flesh hanging in the air for several miles around them, Harrold's stomach churned, a slow blackness descended as he felt himself lose consciousness. What Burke had said now rang in his ears. No one would ever write this soldier's name, except his commanding officer who would try as gently as he could to break the news of his death to the boy's family, telling them that he had died outside of Albert, and that he had fought bravely. They would never know how he died, or what he said in his last moments. Nor would they know the terror which had come from seeing his own body dismembered in a single blast. His body, already torn apart, jarred on a stretcher nearly a quarter mile before succumbing. And he would never again go home except, perhaps, should he not be buried in France, to be placed in the ground.

It was then that Harrold suddenly heard the abject absurdity of somewhere in his mind the lilting refinement of an older woman's voice, one he recognized as that of one of the well-heeled colonial matrons who had toasted him several weeks before upon leaving Muthaiga.

"Remember yourself, Harrold, among all of those hooligans…be sure to return to us when all of this nonsense is over with, when we'll be having tea with the Germans again."

Burke and Harrold sat at the back of the estaminet just outside of the camp on the way toward Amiens. Like the others, Harrold had suffered the indignity of being sprayed with powder and other topical anti-parasitics, having nearly gone pale when he saw what dropped from his body. Even now, freshly clothed and ready to head back to the base, the Englishman had several days' worth of stubble growing on his jaw, his lips cracked and bleeding, and a strange look in his eyes. It was perhaps the only time in his life, Burke mused, in seeing the Englishman's expression, that Harrold hadn't seemed to give a damn about anything, much less his appearance.

Harrold watched the commotion, an older woman and her daughter serving wine while British, French and ANZAC bided their time trying to gain the attention of prospective female companions while singing drunkenly or gambling to blow off steam. The estaminet was small, little larger than a double room, made from one of the barns along the road to several of the larger towns to the west of the line. The two women who were serving drinks and bread must have been the wife and daughter of some elder soldier conscripted into the French Army, the two women having been forced from poverty to turn their property into a weigh station of sorts for Allied soldiers needing comfort from war. For that purpose, local women from within a several-mile radius had also come to meet the soldiers and offer their company for the evening, which to the soldiers only made such a place all the more attractive. It was an unstated meeting of mutual escapism and financial necessity, men and women bent on feeding one another some sense of continuity, however licentious, amidst the chaos.

Burke continued watching Harrold's bitter reverie, at the moment devoid of any satisfaction at the Englishman's discomfort. Harrold had perhaps learned enough from several days on the line to remain silent for a few minutes, perhaps long enough not to write the kind of pretense of which Burke fully expected he was capable when they finally arrived back at the camp.

Harrold grabbed the bottle of wine on the table, pouring more for them both. He then turned, watching the soldiers clicking with unabashed lasciviousness, continuing to pick up the local women, nuances having given way to blatant come-ons, teasing, and drunken professions of love that would quickly be forgotten. He snorted to himself with irritation as he watched one of the women allowing a soldier to touch her breast if only for another drink.

"Here we are, caught in this goddamned hole in the ground, watching women prostitute themselves for a few bloody francs..." He looked at Burke, his tone then suddenly strangely dispassionate. "And you, you bloody bastard, look as though you could give a good goddamn."

Burke watched as the Englishman frowned, downing the glass of wine, now silent, not making any attempt to engage. His face had turned to stone, his expression one Burke had never before seen. But it had been warranted, and predictable, the moment Harrold had arrived in Paris.

The only noticeable movement came from the Englishman when he turned, watching the door open as three new patrons ambled inside. At first, he barely noticed them. He frowned, recognizing the same flash of blonde hair he had seen back at the camp several days before. He lowered his gaze, concentrating enough to see her, dressed in her usual khaki British military fatigues and jacket, her hair now loose in a mane which flowed in thick waves down her back. She walked over to the bar, speaking to the barman, her manner relaxed. She offered him a slow, easy smile as he poured her what looked like a shot of whisky. Several of the men stopped their current seductions to watch her, fascinated as the women in the estaminet shot her both looks of curiosity and contempt. She ignored them, ordering wine for the soldiers with her, nodding in a kind of strangely natural camaraderie, the gentleness of her voice audible across the room.

Harrold nodded to her absently. "Christ..."

Burke raised his head, frowning. He then turned in the direction of the Englishman's gaze.

Harrold nodded toward her. "I noticed she's a surgeon at the camp." Harrold continued, his tone unintentionally lascivious. "She's RAMC, from the patch on her jacket. She must have had some decent connections to be allowed to serve as something other than a nurse at a clearing station."

"She's been on the front since the RAMC set up camp." Burke paused, his voice even. "She's also an

American."

Harrold stared at her, his tone amused, noticing Burke's interest, as he looked at her quietly. "She may be an American, but you'd fuck her if you could," he said, his voice halting. "Christ—so would I."

Burke watched as she again brushed aside several would-be suitors, hard-skins who offered to buy her a drink. Burke could see her warm sense of humor as she joked with the men, even while keeping her distance, apparently knowing better than to engage them past a warm, subtle reserve.

The woman then turned around, looking through the bar as though feeling the distinct gaze of a particular man's eyes. Harrold frowned, watching as she scanned the room silently, and after a moment glancing in their direction and settling on Burke. Harrold watched her in continued fascination as she then stood, excusing herself from her companions before crossing the few feet between the bar and Burke and Harrold's table. They watched her come, her stride smooth and unselfconscious, her agenda less being the obvious gaze of two men than her own curiosity. But soon she stood before them, looking at Burke. Something passed between them which Harrold couldn't discern, as she spoke to him quietly.

"Don't you know, Monsieur, that it's rude to stare?" She then smiled with a warm amusement, seeing his uniform, the harp and crown badge, and the apparent Celtic features on a face which was somewhat familiar to most who had gone through the camp. "Or perhaps you'd prefer I say the same thing in Irish."

Her words were smooth, but deeply pointed, her eyes locked on the Irishman as she waited silently to hear what he would have to say.

Burke smiled slightly to himself. "I didn't realize I was staring."

She glanced at the two glasses half-filled beside each of the men. She picked up the bottle beside Burke, tilting it until she could see that it was nearly empty. She then peered at them, placing the bottle back down. "It's not often a man can find himself in an estaminet like this, with all its distractions, and be coherent enough to carry a conversation."

She looked briefly at Harrold, seeing his dazed expression, as though he realized something of interest were happening. She turned back, gesturing toward the women at the bar. "There are some women here who might be willing to offer you some company, and for much less than the price of a bottle." She then smiled, her voice low. *"Messieurs."*

Then, casting another look in his general direction, she turned, walking back to the bar. After a short word, she nodded to something under the bar, placing enough money down on the bar to cover the entire estaminet's tab. Without looking at them she turned to leave, closing the door behind her.

The bartender came over to them, handing the two men a bottle of expensive Bordeaux, which he had apparently kept hidden for her and which she had apparently just bought for them. He nodded to the door where the American surgeon had just exited. "Compliments de Mademoiselle O'Hanlon."

Harrold sat back. He peered at Burke. The Irishman stared absently across the room as Harrold checked the label. "Cheval Blanc... Quite a good vintage for this hole in the ground."

"You expect anything else from a wealthy American serving for the British, you'd be mistaken."

Harrold paused, taking in the information before he slammed the bottle down harder than he intended, the sound of his laughter carrying through the dilapidated building.

They were back at the camp several hours later, having withstood the ride with several soldiers from the estaminet, the stench of smoke and cheap perfume from the women's clothing still hanging in the air. Any drunkenness, hidden from officers from the Press Office, had slowly begun to subside as Harrold lay on his cot, opening mail he had just received from the censors, who had gone through even the correspondence from his five-year old daughter.

He wondered what his daughter would have thought, had she seen him, now almost unrecognizable, his complexion paled from a lack of food, too many cigarettes, and exposure from having been on the line just hours before. It was not a picture he would have wanted her to see. For days men even in the reserve lines would remain without food, clean water, and any word from the rear, waiting for orders. Harrold had felt as though he had been entombed, the few rays of light which shone into the trenches having been enough to elicit cheers from whole companies of soldiers, as though that alone made their predicament much easier to handle. His daughter had been the only thing that he had been able to think about, watching the soldiers, many of them no more than boys themselves. He remembered her wide oval face in moments when everything had been quiet, thinking that in all of the months since he had been back, in London there was a small child he didn't even know. And here he was watching other men die, men who also had children at home, children, like his, who would miss their fathers during the time they would have been gone and devastated if they never came home again. For years his daughter had been little more than a photograph, as he had been for her. And even so, she had drawn pictures to be included with a terse letter from his wife, asking when he would return from the squalid and unseemly life of a correspondent on the front. It was a position, she wrote as she had before, it seemed he could have refused, asserting that such was his duty as husband and father, as it was to his place among others who had returned from the colonies.

Burke sat quietly, taking a flask from his pocket. He glanced over at the Englishman, seeing a picture his daughter had colored and slipped inside the letter—a colorful depiction of her and his wife, the child holding her mother's hand. The writing above it was the girl's name in the awkward, unsteady hand of a child just learning to write. He knew, having been among a more aristocratic set before, the picture had most likely been included by the nanny rather than Harrold's own wife, as she had only written to him in the last weeks to demand his return home.

Burke looked at it quietly. "You miss them."

Harrold nodded. "My daughter, yes. But knowing my wife, she wishes I'd meet some heroic demise so she could walk around London dressed in black and cause a stir among the ladies at her club." Harrold stared at the photograph of his wife on the small table beside him, propped up along with another of her with his daughter.

"I suppose she has her reasons."

Harrold smirked, realizing that Burke was chiding him, which appealed to his own natural acerbic tendencies. Harrold then nodded, his tone still more subdued. "We were married young—the eldest of two families who saw fit to marry one another to combine both excellent bloodlines and their dwindling fortunes." Harrold then chortled disagreeably. "Besides, all she wanted was children. We had a daughter. Now we're waiting to see if the next one will be a son."

"You should be back in London."

"And wasting time attending endless lunches in the Oxford and Cambridge Club dining room." Harrold then suddenly looked at him. "And how about you? Wife and children?"

"No."

"You've told me nothing at all—much less anything to make you more sympathetic than the blackguard you make yourself out to be." Harrold placed the letter and the picture his daughter had drawn on the small table beside him. He glanced at the Irishman, amusement rising in him as he slowly thought back on the night's events. "You were pretty quiet on the ride back from that estaminet," he said, gauging the Celt's response. "Just making sure you weren't susceptible to a certain surgeon's charms. She was quite beautiful."

"So is every woman in France after a few weeks on the line."

Harrold smiled wryly. "Perhaps I don't know you well, but at some point you're going to realize that despite your experience being a jaded bloody bastard, you're not a very good liar."

Burke frowned, leaning back in his cot, closing his eyes as if to end the conversation, his expression purposefully vacant, as though he would have shown nothing no matter what the Englishman might have said. Harrold watched him for several moments, then chuckling to himself, he blew out the flame in the lantern by his side and settled back in his cot for the few hours before morning.

The camp was finally silent, night having fallen as the soldiers bunked down until dawn, when the transport would again arrive to bring men back or take them out to the front near the Somme. Bonfires were lit, the sparks shooting into the night sky.

Maeve stood silently, looking over the camp. The air was chilled, the vapor from her breath condensing in the night air. After a moment, she bowed her head and entered the infirmary tent, closing the heavy flap behind her to keep the warmth inside.

She paused at the foot of the long rows of cots set up on either side of the tent, tall lanterns lit throughout to maintain the heat. Not a single bed was empty, the soldiers there in various stages of injury, many of them bandaged beyond recognition, resting until they could be moved away from the front to the hospitals and rest stations in Paris.

Maeve walked further into the room, noticing one of the men on whom she had operated only hours before. Something about him drew her to him, and she moved to sit in a chair beside his bed. She watched the soldier in silence. From what she had known of him, he had once been a tall, handsome member of the Scots Guards. Thousands had died in hours, and without having seen him, she knew that reports from the War Office home to his family would suggest he was one of the lucky ones for the simple fact that he was still alive. His face and body had been freshly bandaged perhaps only an hour ago, though new blood even now had stained the dressings, his wounds seeping uncontrollably. According to the reports, a white star shell had exploded near his section, a combination of chlorine and phosgene gas which infected the gashes he had sustained from the accompanying shrapnel. But she had already known, having seen the effects on her table too many times before.

In her periphery she saw the other filled beds, each with a soldier in a similar state of harm. For many of them, there was not much more anyone could do but keep them comfortable until they were either sent to the rear or the deterioration of their bodies would cause them to slip away in silence.

The soldier awakened, his eyes opening slowly. In the soft glow of the room he was soon able to focus on the subtle angles of her face, her hair pulled back, a few gentle waves having escaped to fall across her cheek. She noticed his gaze and smiled gently, as though to comfort him. "I'm sorry—I didn't mean to wake you."

He closed his eyes for a moment, as though battling his morphine-induced drowsiness to speak. His voice came out in a deep whisper. "I thought you had come for me," he said. He peered at her earnestly. "Am I going home soon?"

She smiled softly, in hearing the strong depth of his voice, his words carrying a different meaning than might have otherwise appeared on the surface. She paused, sensing whom he perhaps had once been as a man away from the front, and not just as a soldier. She nodded, speaking to him quietly so as to reassure him. "Soon."

The soldier closed his eyes as she reached over, resting the warmth of her hand on his chest knowing he would soon drift back to sleep.

Maeve watched him for a few moments, waiting until she saw the slowing rise and fall of his chest. She then stood, walking to the entrance to the tent. She lifted the flap and took a few steps before closing it behind her, needing to once again feel the coldness of the air. Whatever emotions she had felt would need to dissipate, lest they become visible to anyone still awake. Beside her she watched several night duty nurses emptying one of the Red Cross supply vehicles that had come in that afternoon, as from inside the next tent, she could hear another tending to a soldier who had been brought in a few hours before. Maeve could hear the tenderness of the nurse's voice as she sang to him softly, comforting him: *"The field is red with poppy flowers, where mushroom meadows stand…it's only seven fairy hours from there to Fairyland…"*

An older nurse passed, pausing as she noticed Maeve listening, her head bowed from exhaustion. The nurse approached her quietly, having overheard Maeve's conversation with the soldier and hoping to offer at least some degree of comfort.

"They always think we're angels come to take them home this time of night," she said gently. "Maybe it's best he won't make it 'til morning."

A few hours later, Maeve stood outside, not yet

wanting to go back to her barracks, adrenaline having coursed through her long enough that she knew she would not be able to sleep. Instead she stood, watching the grooms taking care of several officers' horses from the cavalry tents, brushing them down before dawn. She walked over to one of the horses, watching as it reached for her, its nose nudging her to stroke its face. She smiled, rubbing the wide space between its eyes, feeling the dust which was a contrast to the sterile environment they tried to keep in the surgery, despite the constant stream of chatt-infested men and boys who would find their way to the table. The tactile sensation of something other than injured bodies and hospital instruments was warmly comforting. She inhaled, enjoying the smell the leather of the tack, the oil of the saddle soap, and the musty sweetness of fresh straw. For a few moments, her eyes closed, she could imagine herself anywhere but there, the smells bringing back other visceral memories. She recalled the smell of salt air, damp earth, and the wind brushing against her as she stood at the sea, the last time she had ridden a horse such as this before the war, to spread her father's ashes in his home country after his death.

She remembered having gone to Ireland, facing the cold, churning gray of the Atlantic from the height of black rocks looking west toward the country her father had later called his home, even if it was not the location where he would be placed to rest. He had chosen for his ashes to be scattered near the birthplace of his paternal grandmother, after whom Maeve had been named and whom he had said had also once stood on this same ground from the height of the cliffs, staring down into the sea. Those days before the war were what Maeve had thought about at night, when needing to be somewhere else for those moments, if even in her own mind. It had been for a long time an indelible enough memory to sustain her, those moments being on the very soil where her own family had come from, a daughter bringing her father home. She had watched as his ashes swirled on the currents of the air, and then in the icy gray waters of the ocean, the ocean itself commemorating the bridge between who he once was, and then the man whom he had later become, his one daughter being his chosen emissary in making sure both were remembered.

With the rapidly changing demeanor of industrialized warfare, and having gone from Ireland first to Scotland to study medicine, and then on to the University of Paris for training as a surgeon, she, like those just out of school and trained in the latest surgical techniques as well as briefed in the latest forms artillery, gas and other weapons which were being developed by both sides, would be desperately needed once reaching the front. And, like the others, she had taken on the demeanor of a *chirurgien de guerre*, placing the importance on the men whom she operated on, and spurning anyone who would instead draw attention to the obvious novelty of her presence. Some had seen the rare, if slow, burn of a restrained anger when attention was drawn away from surgery to her sex, though her sudden, and purposeful imposition of command, and the change of expression often rendered whatever perpetrator to the point of apologetic capitulation. It had become clear whether among officers or the corps of surgeons that she belonged, her commitment and talents unmatched, and among those who had worked with her, it was soon understood she was among the best they had. Any other consideration, with the sheer number of casualties, needed to be a veritable afterthought. The only recognition of her gender had been when receiving correspondence from family back home in the States, maiden aunts and those from the more rarefied sides of her family considering it scandalous that in her early thirties she was not only unmarried but had thrown herself into a war the United States wasn't yet even fighting. Having been in Europe, and seeing those she knew going off to war, there had been no question in her mind and, according to her own conscience, there had been no other choice.

Now, as she stood silently, as it was for weeks, and

out of habit from the years used to the surges of adrenaline necessary to keep working even when it seemed impossible, she had barely had more than a few hours of sleep a night. And even if she could have slept, she would have chosen to be on duty to keep from the nightmares that had become common among all who had worked the units. Faces of the dead haunted their sleep as they had among those on the line. Even exhaustion couldn't keep her from rising out of bed in a panic, feeling that she should have been in surgery instead of resting. Even now, she continued to spend what little time during which she didn't sleep doing whatever she could to ease the pressure. And so she was here, now at the cavalry tents in the camp, allowing the distraction of something which had once been one of the joys of her youth, and later, during holidays from school, like any patrician American in Europe, when she had gone with friends to the country, riding for hours as a means of escape. She smiled, thinking about those days, without care, escapism having meant something much different than it did in the few hours, now, when she should have kipped just before dawn.

As she stood, she felt someone behind her. She turned to find the Englishman from the evening before, standing there.

"I'm sorry, I didn't mean to startle you."

She shook her head. "You didn't. I just finished checking everyone for the night," she said quietly. "All the same, I'll need to go to sleep. I'll need to be back in surgery before dawn. No doubt there will be more bodies to work on before morning."

"No doubt," he said, smiling. He joined her by the stall and looked at the horse she had been visiting, seeing the easiness of her posture, and the natural warmth with which she seemed to approach the animal, as though it were a natural extension of herself. "And in the meantime, I take it being among those of an equine persuasion relaxes you."

She nodded. "The officers let me borrow one of

their horses if I need to get away for a while," she said, amused. "It beats playing cards with the other surgeons."

"What game?"

She laughed. "Definitely not the American version of backstreet poker."

He smiled. "And you know such a game."

"I may have been brought up well, but I've been around enough to learn a thing or two."

He nodded, amused, noting the depth of tiredness in her voice, despite her ease and warmth among everyone with whom he had seen her interact. He looked down and noticed the cavalry patch she had had sewn onto her jacket. She followed his gaze and looked at it for a moment, before looking at him again, smiling slightly. "One of the cavalry officers used to play polo in Deauville. He was engaged to a friend when I was in school."

"Trading a mallet for a lance."

She nodded, her voice even. "Like everyone else, he thought the war would last only a matter of weeks."

"What happened to him?"

She bowed her head. "He passed through surgery a year or so ago," she said. "One of the few times I hadn't wanted to see a familiar face. It became apparent pretty quickly it wasn't likely he would see the circuit again."

Harrold remained silent, as he understood, now, all too well the import of her statement.

She then smiled warmly again, as though to reassure him she was fine and his silence understood. She paused, looking across the camp. "So, you must be here for a reason," she said gently. "Though I'd think after several days on the line you'd be catching up on sleep."

"Well, it seems the bloody bastard in the next cot can't sleep without shaking the rafters."

She smiled, nodding. "The Irishman."

"I thought about it, and it seemed inexcusable that we would be in the same camp and I wouldn't introduce myself, especially since you were kind enough to buy us both a rather expensive bottle a few nights ago—one it seems you obviously had been saving for yourself." He smiled, extending his hand. "Harrold Forsythe."

She nodded warmly, shaking it. "Maeve O'Hanlon." She shook her head, remembering the evening before, feeling from the night's events as though it were days ago as opposed to only several hours. She looked at the Englishman, her tone teasing him evenly. "I'm assuming you're not accustomed to some American here among this lot, especially one who knows her wine."

He laughed. "Not under normal circumstances, but then I've had differing experiences among the American contingents. You are a strange lot."

She smiled, sensing as though for her sake he was attempting to alleviate the overwhelming haze of morbidity not just in the air of the surgery, but the front itself. "You have no idea... But then my father was from Armagh. American, but distinctly Irish—and Irish-born. As Irish as the man you're assigned with."

Harrold smiled. "Well, I certainly hope that fact won't keep us from being friends."

She laughed. "My mother is in London as we speak. She would rather have faced zeppelins and be among the British than remember she was once an American debutante married to an Irishman." She paused, seeing his reaction. "But then I assume you're not here about family history." Harrold looked at her quietly. She smiled, seeing his expression. "I don't know, and perhaps it's none of my business, but I thought I'd be jaded enough to never anticipate seeing an Englishman of your station and a man like Burke working alongside each other, even as fellow correspondents."

"We're on the same side in this particular war."

"It's nice to know that's even possible." She reached up, stroking the horse's face. "They're always passing new journalists through here, at least the ones who have managed to get accreditation. From what I understand, they won't let most of you get any closer to the line than maybe a few areas of bombardment. Most of the officers believe they'll keep you immune from any of this, even if it means keeping the real face of war away from the public." She turned slightly, looking over the camp. "Every time I read anything when I'm in town, it's the usual in the newspapers—that brave poilu and Tommies are single-handedly winning the war…and doing so with a smile on their faces. It's no wonder that soldiers refuse to read the papers when they're on leave. And why you might find they're less than friendly to you." She smiled. "Burke especially, as he's as much a champion as they have."

"The same man who is currently shaking the rafters."

Maeve paused, nodding. "He's well known around here—and known for his rather acerbic nature. But it's understandable. Men like Burke covered the front before correspondents were officially allowed on the line. The War Office knew he would be a rogue element—better to accredit him and have him under their wing than running roughshod over their attempts to keep information from the public. They knew that already when the war started. There are few who can get the kind of information he does. The soldiers trust him. And they should. He's been here longer and has known more war than any of them. Enough to know how to get past the censors."

He smiled. "You know a lot for a surgeon."

She smiled, her voice slightly caustic. "I've been here long enough. And men sometimes tend to forget themselves when there are women present. They see far too few friendly faces while they're here." She paused. "It's one of the reasons GHQ doesn't want anyone of the female persuasion too near the front lines. From what I understand, they consider us, including the nurses, too much of a distraction."

Harrold nodded. "Well, apparently a certain Irishman found you fascinating enough when you walked into a room."

She nodded. "Maybe to you, in from the colonies, describing the typical roughshod Celt with the heart of a poet. That's something I know all too well." She paused, her voice wryly warm. "But I doubt he'd be too pleased if you're here try to play Cupid for him."

A nurse suddenly stepped outside the tent, locating Maeve. Maeve nodded to her and turned toward the infirmary. Several nurses stood over one of the patients, trying to comfort him as he suddenly awakened, writhing from pain. She turned back to Harrold.

"I hope you'll forgive me, Harrold, but I have a patient I should see before I turn in. I may not sleep much, but I should when I can."

He nodded, seeing the nurses looking anxiously in their direction.

Almost as though sensing his thoughts, she smiled. "I wouldn't worry," she said gently. "I'm sure we'll run into one another again." She shook his hand, smiling with genuine kindness as she moved away slowly. "Good night, Harrold."

"Good night."

Harrold stood watching her return to the tent, only turning away once the flap closed behind her.

∞

The extensive line of trench on the front was seven to eight feet wide, running in jagged formation for miles. Soldiers anticipating the German advance rested just before dawn, some of them wide awake, waiting on the fire-steps of the front line, their rifles poised on stand-to for the call to fire. They stared through fencing and barbed wire for any sign of movement, while working parties repaired several pickets, fixing the position as a couple of sharpshooters covered them from behind. Others waited in the dugouts, smoking and drinking from their provisions, while others who had been on sentry duty ate tinned beef and biscuits infamous among infantry for being hard enough to nail pickets, though comparably more savory than some of the other rations offered by the British army. Each man bided his time, knowing that at any moment the silence would be shattered by the sound of German mortars, with the front line soon going over the top of front trenches, moving headlong into heavy fire.

Burke sat quietly, watching, hearing nothing but the uncomfortable silence and the few soldiers who whispered to one another several feet away. Like the others, he was poised in the darkness, his body tense, ready to move at a moment's notice. Harrold was silent beside him, rigid from tension, and despite himself, his heart pounding. For the last few hours he had tried to pretend as though none of it affected him, being so close to no-man's-land, filled with the fear of one who had never been so close to any area of direct bombardment. He could almost feel the charge in the air, the knowledge that perhaps less than a few hundred yards away, there were howitzers fixed on their positions. Aircraft had flown overhead the day before, their engines sputtering and whining as their pilots marked Allied positions all the way down the line. Within moments, front line attacks would begin, targeting those areas suggested by the previous day's intelligence, and those who weren't hit by the first barrage would soon be heading over the trench, moving past their own demarcations straight into enemy fire. All Harrold would be able to do was steel himself for the action which he knew would inevitably follow, watching engagement from several hundred yards away and praying like hell they wouldn't sustain the same damage to the line as others who were more directly in danger of being hit by artillery. It was enough that Burke had been able to get them this close to the front line, which had been a feat unto itself and must have come from more than some gentle persuasion. But as anyone who had never been in such a position, it had been impossible to anticipate what it would actually feel like. Such fear was more than palpable and felt to the bone to an extent he had never believed possible, as once again, he could feel his stomach churning. He couldn't have been alone in his fear, no matter how jaded, insane, or dispassionate any one of the men must have seemed. They were just more used to it, and perhaps, too busy to entertain it as their only interest at this point, in addition to whatever military objective had been ordered by command, was to stay alive.

Burke touched him on the shoulder, nodding to the forward sap, where several soldiers were on lookout for any enemy movement. One of them had affixed a mirror to his bayonet with twine to look over the parapet, sighting a segment of the German trenches. Burke watched as the soldier moved it carefully, saying a silent prayer.

The darkness began to lift, and the soldier lowered the mirror, not wanting it to catch the first rays of sunlight and reflect anything across the desolate, deep-pitted stretch of no-man's-land. Burke could see the soldiers' eyes fixed on a point in the distance, their bodies tensed and shivering from the coldness of the dawn and the adrenaline which waited to explode through their bodies. Burke turned to Harrold who was blowing on his hands to keep them warm.

"No action yet," Harrold said, trying to hide his nervousness.

Burke shook his head. "There won't be. They'll wait until first light before they engage the line." He frowned. "They'll send storm troops first, flanking our positions with short-range artillery. Then infantry will move forward in a creeping barrage. Field artillery will cover them from behind."

Harrold heard a shout, one of the dugout soldiers turning toward the rest of the men on the line as the scream of a mortar suddenly found its target down the line, the blast shattering the silence. Within moments, a field officer called to the troops, commanding them to stand ready.

Burke muttered. "Must be dawn."

Several more mortars suddenly blasted through the line nearby, creating huge indentations in the ground near the forward sap, blasting through the wire and sending earth in every direction. The Allied soldiers moved up to the firewall in a matter of seconds, crouching and taking cover until they were ordered to head over the trench. In the sudden cacophony, an officer screamed over the heads of the soldiers, ordering one of the reserve companies to come from the rear, sending a runner through the communications trench. Several of the soldiers prepared to shoot tracers across the heavy mist hovering over the ground between trenches when the barrage was finished, as the landscape for the most part was still shrouded in darkness.

"Stay back. If they engage this part of the line, and the ready order is called, let them move first, then head back to the communications trench and wait. Whatever you do, stay out of their way. If shrapnel from one of the mortars doesn't kill you, something else will. When they figure they've done enough damage, they'll cease the medium-range guns and begin their advance. That's when one of the field officers will order the first company of soldiers over the line."

Harrold stared at him as another shout was suddenly heard, followed by the deafening thunder of artillery moving ever closer to their position. After several rounds, a new series of explosions carried over no-man's-land, slicing through the air with high-pitched screams, exploding in the enemy's trenches. Several of the soldiers near the reporters stood anxiously, their eyes sharp as they single-mindedly focused on a position where they could negotiate the firing step. They looked as though their senses were heightened to the point of surreality, their reason now completely overtaken by the instinct that would, again, perhaps, keep them alive.

Suddenly a shell landed a few feet away, blasting

through the wire to the parapet, sandbags blown apart, needle-like grains of sand showering them from every direction as the field commander ordered the advance. In the near distance, Harrold watched as companies of men charged past the trench, shooting into the incoming mortars and gunfire, the sound reaching a fever pitch. From their position just above the salient, he could see dead bodies and empty artillery shells already littering the muddy field, rats scurrying from the shelled trenches as the men withstood the noise and backlash of incoming fire. They were being flanked, and further than had been expected, leaving their portion of the line in the direct line of fire, which it was apparent Burke had already anticipated.

Harrold tried to hide the sudden paralysis that threatened to seize him, causing him to remain frozen as Burke instinctively moved forward. In the next moment, there was a sudden blast, a canister of poison gas exploding several feet away. Burke stared at it as though it were in slow motion, seeing the yellow cross on the shell as it exploded upon impact.

Burke turned, seeing that others had also seen the shell burst, immediately putting on their gas masks. Burke addressed Harrold gruffly, his face contorted as he tried to make himself heard over the din. "Put on your mask!"

Harrold put the mask over his head, watching as the other soldiers, not already shell-shocked, do the same. Others who were lying wounded did not, not able to keep themselves from breathing in, choking and sputtering as their skin turned color, the chemical reaction from the sudden haze making contact with their windpipes and every exposed inch of skin. Burke called angrily to Harrold as Harrold remained frozen, his breath coming fast in short bursts as the panic began to hit.

Burke yelled, shoving him roughly. *"Forsythe—get the fuck back behind the line!"*

Harrold turned, seeing the mass of soldiers from a reserve company donning masks and moving forward, pulling wounded from the area before the wire. He backed away, hearing his own voice cry out as he watched a bullet blast suddenly through his shoulder, ripping through his flesh as it exited on the other side, the explosion slamming him back against the floor of the trench. His shoulder searing in pain, he closed his eyes, feeling the blood spurting down his arm into the heaviness of the mud, his body sinking as soldiers continued to move around him, screaming into the oncoming fire. Burke ran to cover him and, wasting no time, tightened a makeshift bandage around the wound with a piece of his jacket he had torn off of his own body. Within moments, the wound would have begun to burn from the mustard gas permeating the air. Burke fell back against the trench, wall, pausing for a moment before he got them both back toward the traverse that would take them to the rear lines.

Maeve moved quickly a few miles away, barking orders, pointing nurses to meet stretcher-bearers and instruct them where to put the latest group of men who were being brought in, while heading off to another operation in one of the six surgical units waiting for casualties. Maeve paused to examine an incoming soldier who had sustained massive burns and blistering from mustard gas.

"How long since exposure?"

"Several hours, Ma'am. We just got him from the dressing station—"

She cursed, moving away to check on another patient as more transports arrived, the drivers screaming at the infirmary attendants to move the collection of wounded out of the way. *"Too goddamn many—"*

Other soldiers were brought in, a mass of confusion among the multiple cases, many of which appeared hopeless, everyone covered with blood, soot, powder and dirt. Emergency operations commenced, often without anesthetic, as there was no time to administer it before getting another living, if shattered body, on the table, screams ringing out as scalpels and other instruments dug into already charred flesh, morphine and ether having run low days before.

A nurse called loudly to Maeve, nodding toward the door. "Ma'am—you have a couple of men here to see you who just came from the line."

Maeve glared toward the doorway, seeing no one. She turned back to the soldier she had been evaluating, working on him with another of the surgeons, watching as he remained unconscious while the other surgeon extracted another piece of shrapnel from the soldier's chest.

"Captain…"

A man's hand touched her shoulder. She turned to find the chief surgeon as he addressed her gently by rank as he would have any other surgeon in the RAMC. She knew how she must appear to him— pale, having been in surgery without pause for over twenty hours, as with most of the other surgeons, not having eaten or slept, as always, continuing to operate on sheer adrenaline, enough to take on another patient. He addressed her gently, knowing she would resist him ordering her to stop. Then, in heavily-accented English, "Maeve, you're one of the best we have…but as much as you may want to, you can't save them all." He smiled. "Go take care of your friends. And when you've had a chance to rest, I'll need you back."

She stared at him, watching him plead silently for her to step back. Her jaw tightening as she nodded bitterly, to no one in particular, setting the instruments down on the table beside them. She looked down at herself, seeing that she was dripping with sweat, blood spattered over her clothing. The chief surgeon watched her walk out through the doorway, tearing off her heavy surgical apron and tossing it in exhaustion and frustration to the floor.

Maeve paused against a pile of sandbags being loaded

quickly onto an awaiting vehicle. She dropped her head against her chest, breathing deeply, her body rigid as she wiped the blood from her forehead with the back of her hand. She trembled in the cold, adrenaline still coursing through her as she watched the commotion of the camp in the dank, freezing morning air, the camp clouded in a frozen mist, punctuated by the glow, every few feet, of soldiers' campfires. She could hear the sirens, and the sounds of long-range guns in the distance. She paused, watching the silhouette of two men heading for one of the surgical units. Maeve started silently, heading toward them.

Harrold walked forward from the transport shouldered by Burke, a seeping wound dressed haphazardly on his shoulder, his breath visible in the cold air. Maeve approached them, immediately taking some of the weight from Burke as she held him from the other side.

"What the hell happened?"

"He caught a bullet in the shoulder. They sutured it at the dressing station."

Harrold snorted at the irony in Burke's voice and grimaced, his teeth clenched despite himself. "That's one way to put it."

"Where were you?"

"Near Albert."

Maeve turned to Burke, her voice cold. "And you didn't stay on the line?"

Burke remained silent as she led them into a smaller reserve tent, filled mostly with medical supplies as well as a couple of beds for surgeons who wouldn't make it back to their barracks. Maeve turned up one of the gas lamps, watching as the tent brightened and warmth began moving through the chilled air. She handed Burke a blanket for Harrold before heading over to the door.

"—Put this on him in case he goes into shock. It hasn't fully hit him yet."

"Where are you going?"

"I need something from surgery."

Burke nodded.

Maeve left the room, heading back to the surgical unit as Harrold snickered, seeing that the Irishman had remained coolly silent. "That was rather... harsh."

Burke frowned. "I think I can handle it."

Harrold felt himself pale, watching the blood continue to soak his dressings. "Christ...what was I thinking following you to the line. How the hell did you know where the assault would come, anyway?"

Burke remained silent.

Maeve came back in, opening her kit and pulling from it a pair of scissors to take off Harrold's dressing. "So—what did they do to you at the dressing station?"

Harrold watched her remove his shirt, clipping away his bandage to reveal the wound which was encrusted with dried blood, the stitches uneven, leaving a gap which now oozed with fresh blood.

"How does it look?"

"You'll have one hell of a scar to tell stories about when you get home."

Harrold grumbled deeply, feeling his skin flush with pain. "I can't wait."

Maeve sponged the area gently, examining him more closely, clearing both dried and new blood as both Burke and Harrold watched. Harrold closed his eyes as though to not pay attention. She smiled at his reaction, as though it were what she would have expected. "It passed clean through...no bone fragments, or else they would have had to operate on you, and you'd be down for at least a couple of weeks..." She paused. "Or maybe you would have preferred being sent home?"

"Not bloody likely."

Burke chortled, watching as Maeve cleaned the wound, looking for suppuration as she doused it with iodine.

"You're lucky...if it had hit bone it would have done some damage. Looks like the wound came from a 98—an 8mm bolt-action Mauser—probably some German grunt got hold of it, not realizing it's often used as a sniper's rifle, particularly if it was missing its sights. If a sniper had hit you, you'd be dead by now." She shook her head, irritated. "The bullet wasn't deflected, so they should never have sutured the wound...it would have healed on its own. You don't faint at the sight of blood, do you, Harrold?"

Harrold opened his eyes, frowning, between pain and irritation at the insult of the suggestion, and soundly amazed that she could extrapolate the model of gun and caliber of shell which had been used to trounce him.

Maeve dabbed at the wound again to clean it, making him wince. "You're going to have to hold your breath while I re-suture this—at this point I don't have much of a choice, considering the damage they've already done to the tissue in suturing it the first time. It won't heal properly unless I clean it again. So, as I do, I suggest you drink everything you've got in that flask." She pulled out a surgical needle, threading it expertly. Harrold looked down at it, registering its size. Maeve glanced at him, her voice calm. "Once I'm done, if the wound becomes pulpy, or you see the skin start to form a gray, opalescent membrane around it, come back and I'll use iron perchloride, which is going to hurt like hell, but it will cauterize the wound where the surface of the skin has become gangrenous." She paused, her voice even. "You're lucky—these days surgeons would rather cut limbs off than take the chance they'll become infected. Can't have you losing an arm, Forsythe, or it might keep you from writing."

Burke watched Harrold suddenly pale as the import of her suggestion fully reached him, immediately transcending any further curiosity. Within moments he had slowly fallen back against the cot. "Christ..."

Maeve laughed. "Well, I guess that takes care of whether or not you'll be in pain." She raised an eyebrow, continuing to clean the wound, knowing he could hear her, as much as he was attempting to ignore everything and everyone else. "A rugged English colonial from Nairobi, whom I'd guess should be used to staring down lions and other predators in the bush." She paused, amused. She looked at Burke. "But then, Harrold, you seem like a good one…" she said, smiling. "Which I'm saying despite what I'd hope is better judgement."

Harrold sputtered, trying not to wince from pain. "He doesn't give a damn. If anything, he's goddamned well enjoying every moment of this."

She laughed, placing her hand gently on Harrold's as he again closed his eyes. Burke smiled slightly despite himself as he watched her suture the wound, her hands moving quickly, sewing back together the flesh on either side of his shoulder.

"He's still out."

Maeve walked over to Burke, looking through the doorway to the infirmary, seeing Harrold still unconscious, lying underneath the covers of the rough wool blanket she had placed over him, having given him some morphine so that he'd fall asleep. She looked at Burke quietly, frowning as she touched his shoulder and found a rip in his shirt she hadn't noticed before. Burke looked down as Maeve examined the flesh, seeing blood congealing against a wound where a shell
fragment had grazed his shoulder.

"It's nothing."

"Usually nurses take care of this, but I'm here, and it will turn septic if you don't let me take care of it," she said reaching for a bottle of iodine. "If I'm any judge of character, my tactics aren't about to work on you, so take off your shirt so I can get a better look." She then smiled. "I'm as stubborn as you are, Burke. You won't know what else I may have up my sleeve."

Burke unbuttoned his shirt slowly, his thick eyebrow raised in irritation as she watched him, readying a cotton patch doused with red-brown salt solution. He barely winced as she touched where the bullet had grazed him.

"You'd rather take care of an injured friend than get your story, even if it means getting injured yourself. I'm sorry for what I said." She then paused, bowing her head for a moment, as though considering what she should say next. "And, too—about what happened in town. Until I talked with Forsythe, I never realized I made such an impression."

He looked at her quietly. "Unless that was your intention. Not too many surgeons around like you. Or women like you for that matter."

Maeve cleaned the wound as Burke sat, her voice becoming matter of fact as she continued speaking. "I lost ten soldiers today," she said absently. "One of them came in, holding onto his own leg which had been blasted off by a mine. He wouldn't let anyone touch it. The only time we could pry it from him was after he was already dead." Burke remained silent. She smiled bitterly, as she finished in seconds, moving to dress the wound. "I'd challenge any one of those sonsofbitches back home to withstand even a day watching grown men be reduced to tears, praying to God to save them. But then, you've seen them in the trenches. You know what I'm talking about. There's no real anesthetic—no matter what anyone tries—to ease that kind of pain."

Burke reached over, touching her face gently, wiping a drop of blood from her jaw. She started at first, not knowing what he was doing. She then looked at him quietly, seeing his expression.

"Blood doesn't complement you. Even for a surgeon."

She sat back, having finished. "Forsythe came to see me a few nights ago. He thought I might be susceptible to a man like you, despite what happened at that estaminet near Amiens." She then paused, looking at him. "I figured if you had some kind of message to impart, you would have done it yourself."

He remained silent for several moments, then, "I'm going into town tomorrow. I need to file our stories with the wire service."

Maeve nodded. "I'll look in on him in the morning."

Several moments passed as the two lingered. Then Maeve turned, walking back toward the door. She paused almost despite herself before continuing outside. Burke watched her as she dropped the flap of the tent behind her without looking back.

Burke stood in line with the other journalists in the noisy wire agency, each waiting to telegraph their stories to the Press Office. Most were younger men, laughing and arguing, telling stories and commenting on the latest news and gossiping about the varying commanders poised to be in charge of the incoming American divisions, though with a few exceptions because of the nature of the German onslaught, Pershing had continued to insist on a primarily unified American force under his own command.

Already over a hundred thousand American soldiers had entered training camps near Étaples, others having entered only certain engagements, including the U.S. Second Division which had been inserted among Duchêne's poilu divisions near the Chemin des Dames ridge. Another U.S. Division, the Twenty-Sixth "Yankee" Division had engaged the Germans at Seichprey, near St. Mihiel.

Burke was silent amidst the laughter and commentary, ready to get out of the office once finally given leave to head back to the base. He shook his head, listening to them chatter on about the British, French, and American forces, knowing none of them would have been to the forward lines to see any one of the armies in action, instead, like most of the journalist corps, billeted in the rear. Even their laughter sounded hollow, as much as their commentary— commentary he tried to ignore as he handed over his report. He stared at it as the attendant readied it, seeing it was already censored. Several older reporters recognized him and greeted him as he walked past, recognizing his roughshod appearance and the jaded, intense look in his eyes. They were the few among the others whom he greeted, shaking their hands warmly, but his mind continued to be on something else, something which seemed to move through him with greater intensity every moment he was away from the line.

Several miles away, Maeve watched as the medics brought in another soldier and lifted him onto the table. Shaking and covered in blood, his eyes were wide with terror, his breath coming fast as he began to panic seeing the thick, clotting blood coming from the wounds in his chest. The searing pain of his wounds had rendered him unconscious several times since he had first been taken from the line, having lain for several hours before a stretcher bearer could get to him. He had lost far too much blood, his temperature dropping rapidly, the surgeons at the dressing station having already given him injections of ether to stabilize him. Maeve looked at him quietly, despite herself smoothing the hair back from his muddied forehead as though to comfort him. Seeing her and the strange look in her eyes, a nurse moved over from one of the other patients and immediately began whispering to him gently, comforting him. She looked down, noting his all too familiar injuries, mostly from shell fragments and exposure to combinations of phosgene and mustard gas. Maeve turned to her, her voice low. "Don't give him any more anesthetic. His temperature is too low. And bring that light over here when you can. We need to pull him through, and we're sure as hell not going to do that in the dark."

The nurse nodded.

They heard several more transports arriving outside, nurses and medics yelling for assistance, bloodied bodies placed on the last few tables, the others left writhing on stretchers on the ground with the relentless demand for space and a quickening shortage of chloroform.

Maeve had already dressed in her apron and had begun extracting the scorched shards of metal, the nurse nearby administering doses of carbolic acid to clean the wound, as there was no longer any iodine. Her eyes stung as she stared down, feeling the sweat and blood beading across her forehead as she began repairing the damage. Already she could see that the skin had become discolored and burned, his esophagus and windpipe raw from exposure, the tissue in his lungs disintegrating slowly as he lay unconscious. Like the others she had seen already that day, it was only a matter of time.

She allowed herself to raise her head for a moment, her neck straining. Across the room was an endless line of bodies, several of them shaking violently from wounds and shell shock. Some sat alone, not hurt except for a few scratches, grown men whose eyes seemed wild, strange, frightened noises erupting from them, as though unable to stop their bodies and minds shuddering from what they had just experienced. Nurses moved among the other patients, ones who would go into surgery if they survived the wait, each his own depiction of horror. She stared at them silently for a moment, feeling a tightness form in her chest, then a fire that coursed through her body, her muscles straining from ceaseless hours on her feet. She looked over at one of the other medical officers, he also worked amidst the men who continued to come in without pause, the Germans having fired upon a salient near Albert in retribution for the Allied attacks the previous morning. From what she had seen, they had hit an entire division with hundreds of shells of gas, and others meant to be used as explosives, the short-range artillery hammering any visible post across less than a mile of ground. The wounded had come in enough numbers that they were low on just about every imaginable supply, Ludendorff having made sure to shower the fields in further unmitigated carnage. And this soldier was the latest among them, now unconscious, waiting for her to make another in a series of incisions that may or may not save his life. Maeve closed her eyes for a moment, willing herself to continue as she once again cut into the soldier's flesh, trying not to look into his face.

An hour later she stood beside her a clerk from BEF command. She stared at the boy's form, the same one on whom she had operated only moments before. His skin was pale in a death pall, areas where he had been cracked open or where she had extracted shrapnel now sutured. Each death required reports from the surgeons to command on what forms of gas and artillery had been used, in case it helped them plan their own attacks. For weeks with ever-increasing bombardments, they each had been reporting on his own casualties almost as soon as they had died on the table, the nurses having taken dictation as they stood over bodies of men who perhaps even moments before had been alive, there having been almost not enough time before needing to move on to another wounded body.

Maeve stared at the boy quietly. There was nothing akin to staring into the faces of men whom they had once tried to save, faced with the realization that fate, lack of time or supply had meant another body being sent home. She could feel her own body now become wearied, having taken that one moment to see the boy's face. That sight alone caused the adrenaline to immediately dissipate, her body hurting from both the hours without pause and the import that all of that time, she hadn't been able to save him, among some of the others. It was only within his last moments that he had succumbed, a piece of unseen shrapnel having gone into his brain, cutting off the blood supply enough to cause his body to begin shutting down. It was then that all she wanted was to lie down and close her eyes, not thinking about anything, and not feeling the emotions that coursed through her in such moments. The weeks on end were taking their toll, and more so in having to hear the causes of death she and any other surgeon had been unable to combat.

She bowed her head, listening as the clerk read what she had spoken to a nurse only moments before.

"Case 641, Died 1:32 am. Postmortem report subsequent. Cause, aneurism amidst critical brain tissue. Metal fragment entering through left ocular cavity. Additional acute exposure to mustard gas and chloropicrin, with extensive diphtheritic necrosis of the trachea and bronchi, characteristic of peribronchial reaction. Reports of forward area shelled with Yellow and Green Cross shells. Trench fever present from lice infestation. Evidence of a prolonged stay in gas contaminated shell holes. Burns on the face, scalp, axilla, and scrotum. Interior of lungs shows alternating areas of edema and congestion. Eyes swollen, upon opening, cloudiness of the cornea on one side, with rupture of ocular tissue, as previously reported. Epidermis around the mouth and nose showing crusts from gas burns. The lymph glands are enlarged and edematous, with the bronchus showing ulceration. Extensive hemorrhaging in the lungs, particularly in the upper lobe. Multiple lacerations in evidence to the surface of the skin from silica and shrapnel. These are additional factors of the preceding casualty." He looked up from the report and muttered, "Seems he was quite a mess."

Maeve, too exhausted for sarcasm, looked at the clerk quietly. Registering her irritation, he quickly left the tent. She bowed her head, taking the sheet at the boy's feet and raising it over his body.

A few hours later, Maeve stood in the doorway at sunset, taking in the clearness of the sky as darkness began to fall. She ran a hand through her hair, moving it off her face. Several transports arrived as she stood, soldiers jumping out from the back. Seeing that there were no more bodies, she turned back around, nodding to one of the other surgeons who had come to relieve her as she finished for the night.

She walked into her quarters, a section of the surgeon's barracks which had been partitioned off so that she would have her own tent away from the others. She paused at the entrance to the small room which was filled with a few stray books, all of which were old, frayed from wear and from extensive reading, as she had been unable to sleep soundly for weeks.

Maeve undressed, taking off her shirt, which was soiled from surgery. Each movement was automatic, without thought, as though she had done the same thing a million times before. Each moment away from surgery was left with little emotion as had been a necessity, the backlash of the past hours not reaching her until she had finally allowed herself to lie down, exhaustion having kept any extraneous thoughts from rising to the surface. She walked over to a basin on a table in the corner, pouring water into it. She took a piece of cotton cloth, wiping the stains from her arms, neck and face. Her skin was sallow in the candlelight, the circles under her eyes more pronounced than she had seen them for weeks. She stared into her own eyes for several moments, resisting the desire to turn away, not liking what she saw. She had become thinner over the last months, her strong body now looking pale and hollow. She reached up, placing her hand on the back of her neck, rubbing the tendons to relax the tension which had rested there for weeks. In doing so, she saw that the thin cotton of her camisole was soaked with blood. As she took it off, she caught herself again in the light of the mirror, reflecting the light from the lamp behind her. In the soft glow, a strange chill ran through her as she followed the curves of her body.

It had been months since she had looked at herself, seeing something other than the exhaustion which had usually shone in her eyes. She reached up again, this time touching her face, the angles of her jaw, the skin along her neck. Emotion suddenly rose in her, as though the simple feeling of the skin of her own body responding caused some human part of her suddenly began to awaken, the sensation moving through her slowly. She closed her eyes for several moments, allowing the foreignness of the feeling to linger, perhaps even longer than it should or else have to consign it back to the intentionally forgotten place from which it had come. For months she had not thought of herself as a woman, the human part of her allowed to exist only so far as it allowed her to comfort men who might only need a kind word to convince them to stay alive. Anything else would have been a distraction, or so she told herself during the long hours of the night when she had lain awake, listening to the sounds of the camp. Nothing else was important. The only reason for her presence was as another surgeon attempting to save men who would otherwise be considered the walking dead, as that was all she had ever allowed herself to believe.

She opened her eyes again, staring at her reflection. She reached up slowly, running her hands through her hair, taking it down from where she had tied it behind her. It fell gently against the her naked shoulders, its softness causing her to bow her head, a wave of emotion suddenly moving through her. She could feel the sob rising in her throat, and within moments, she had put her shirt back on and left her tent.

She approached the officers' mews, seeing one of the soldiers sitting, reading by lamplight. She breathed deeply, her body shivering in the coldness of the night, blood pumping mercilessly through her as she stood silently, waiting until he noticed her. When he raised his head, he saw the American surgeon nodding toward him, as though asking silently that he let her pass. He motioned over toward the far end of the mews.

Maeve walked through the mews silently, stopping beside one of the stalls. There she saw her horse, an Irish draught well over seventeen hands. The horse stretched forward, as it had nights before, with its muzzle to touch her shoulder, recognizing her. She stroked his white neck lightly, resting her forehead against him, feeling the warmth and softness of the large animal as she closed her eyes.

Moments later, she had the draught saddled and bridled, walking it from the mews outside. The soldier watched her mount smoothly, her expression indicating that her mind was already elsewhere, on some thought which had possessed her as she gathered the reins in her hands. In the distance, she could see the sun setting, the last orange-red streaks of light visible over the horizon. Within moments, she had moved the horse from the mews, and no one watching, a sob still in her throat as she broke the draught into a gallop, her hair, like the horse's, streaming in a thick mane behind her.

An hour later, Burke arrived back at the base, hauling his pack from the rear as he started toward his barracks. Several other soldiers had come with him, but he paid no attention as he moved through the camp. It was relatively quiet for a change, with no new ambulances arriving or troops moving out until morning. Even the clearing station seemed quiet, with the glow of paraffin lamps seeping through the canvas of the infirmary tents. He looked through one of the open flaps. Nurses moved among the patients, most of the men asleep. The few surgeons on duty sat outside, waiting in case any medical transports came in. He did not see her there and decided that she must be back in her own barracks resting for the night.

A group of soldiers standing by a fire were distracted by something across the camp. He turned and, like the others, saw the dust being kicked up and the sound of hooves in the distance. In the haze of the night, the camp lit by firelight, he saw her long dust-streaked mane flowing with that of the horse, as though they were a single animal. The sight of her caused the men to stop what they had been doing, watching as though she and the horse were some specter riding in from the mist, the horse's mouth open hard against the bit and head bowed, its coat glistening in sweat. They rode in from the west, from the wasteland burned and razed from months of German occupation several months before, as though racing from some unseen apocalypse. Burke watched her from a distance, within moments seeing her clearly enough to notice her face covered in dust as she prodded the horse forward, reaching the edge of the camp, lost in some world which it seemed no one would be able to reach. She disappeared after several moments, the sound of the horse's hooves still reverberating through the relative silence and the sound of soldiers' camp fires, soldiers watching as she disappeared back toward the officers' mews.

Burke stared after her, his breath shallow, slowly realizing what was happening to him as the sound of hoof beats faded into the distance.

Maeve had been gone for almost an hour by the time she pulled the horse up and dismounted, her hands and body shaking as she dropped from the hardness of the saddle to the ground. The same soldier approached her gently, taking the reins from her hand. She looked at him in silence, her face glistening with sweat. He watched as she self-consciously bowed her head, not wanting the soldier to see her eyes. The draught rested its head against her chest. She breathed, smelling the combination of smoke and sweat, as she turned, her eyes burning from more than the campfires a few feet away.

"Can you walk him?" she asked quietly.

He looked the horse over, seeing him lathered in sweat, his white coat glistening. He nodded, knowing she needed to get away from anyone who might have seen her.

"Of course, Ma'am. Leave him to me."

She moved from the horse, placing her hand for a moment, uncomfortable, on the boy's shoulder, thanking him without speaking.

The soldier watched as she moved away, walking across the ground, her breath visible in the night air, her body, only covered in muddy breeches and her bloodied shirt, trembling slightly as she headed back to her barracks.

Another soldier walked up, handing his friend a drink before he began walking the officer's horse. "What was that about?"

"O'Hanlon. The Major lets her ride any time she wants."

The other soldier laughed, his tone crudely suggestive. "I wonder how the bloody hell she managed that."

The sergeant frowned. "Bugger off...after surgery, she doesn't need a reason."

Back in her tent, Maeve sat on her cot, bowing her head, feeling the movement of air against her skin, her body shaking. She breathed deeply, her jaw tensing. She looked in the mirror, seeing herself, her hair still falling in thick waves down her back. She saw the streaks, then, too, from the sweat which had fallen from her face, and the bloodstains which remained on her clothing. She stared, unblinking at her reflection.

But there was something else.

Something on the long table beside her cot caught her eye. A book had been placed so that she would easily see it. She frowned, touching the dark fabric of the book's cover before she reached down to hold it lightly in her hands. The material was worn, as though it had come from someone who had kept it with him in his pocket on the line. She paused, her hands shaking. She opened the book silently to what she saw was a marked page. An eerie sensation moved through her as she looked down, seeing the passage she knew she had been meant to see. In her mind she could hear the deep half-brogue of a man's voice as she read the words, their strange resonance moving through her, without warning, coming to rest heavily in her chest.

> *I dteas na hansachta má táim ag lonrahm*
> *Duitse thar aon ghrá dá dtaibhsíonn ar domhan duit*
> *I slí is go bhfaighim cloíte cumhacht do shúl leis*
> *Ó radharc thar barr atá le foghlaim oilte*
> *Chun siúl ar aghaidh i slí na maithe d'fhoghlaim.*
> *Is maith a chím mar tá t'intlíochtsa tuilte*
> *Den niamh a lasas inti ón solas síoraí*
> *A adhnas i gcónaí grá gan ach é a d'fheiscint...*

> *If with the flame of love I shine beyond*
> *The measure that is seen on Earth and overwhelm*
> *The power of your eyes, be not astonished, since*
> *The reason is my perfect sight, which as it apprehends*
> *Moves closer to the apprehended good.*
> *For in your intellect I clearly see already shining*
> *The Eternal Light, which when it has been seen*
> *Is such that it alone and always lights the fire of love.*

Emotion moved through her, she turned, looking through the narrow separation of the flap of her tent, as though looking straight to the press barracks.

Burke stood outside, watching Maeve's silhouette, the soft glow of her oil lamp lit beside her, which he could imagine casting shadows onto her face. The wind had begun howling outside, moving across the ground. He watched her as she stood slowly and moved toward the flap of the doorway. After a moment, she lifted it and saw him outside. She paused, watching him as he stood silently. Rain had begun to fall, the drops now striking gently against his clothing. She stepped back slowly, allowing him to come inside and closed the flap behind him. He then looked down, seeing the book in her hands. She waited for several moments, watching him standing before her, the surprise of an enigmatic expression on his face, which she knew mirrored her own.

"Why did you leave this for me?"

He nodded over to her table, indicating her collection of books, well-read and worn, their numbers stacked by her bed. "I know you read to pass the time."

She nodded. "And this passage."

Burke looked at her quietly, hearing the smooth depth of her voice. He then looked in the direction of the surgery, pausing before he turned back to her, looking with a raw, unguarded ferocity straight into her eyes. "Maybe because I knew you would understand."

She stared at him for a moment, then despite herself bowed her head, unable to look at him. He moved toward her, any hesitation gone as he reached to touch her face. She could feel the warmth of his hand even before he touched her skin. Chills ran through them both as he could feel her trembling, the warmth of her skin rising in goose flesh underneath his fingers, responding with a strength that surprised him.

He paused, looking again into her face as he raised it to meet his. He had longed to touch her these past months, to feel the warmth which he knew resided in more than her eyes, which had been, for so long, like her voice, the only thing she had allowed anyone else to know. It was as though she had seen into him every time she had looked into his eyes, knowing every thought, every emotion which resided there, without speaking, as he had within her. The experience had been torturous— neither had been able to guard themselves, both so used to being impenetrable out of necessity, not allowing any emotion to reach them which would have made them vulnerable. But over the past weeks, she had been all he had been able to think about, the soul who was beautiful and impenetrable, but underneath whatever defenses she had erected, still human.

Without taking her eyes from his, as though reading his mind, she reached up to touch his hand, her fingers entwining in his, feeling their warmth against her skin, the roughness of him scarred and strong against the softness of her flesh, like her carrying the marks of war, the experience of someone's life slipping away while covered in soldiers' blood. He lingered, his hands in hers, his eyes glistening.

He could feel the warmth of her before him, both of them barely breathing, a strange pain moving through them, as though the distance had slowly become tortuous. It was a depth of emotion neither had ever felt, the uncontainable warmth, an ache rising within them, as though the pain of a sudden void had become deeply known, and in those moments had disappeared. He drew her to him. Her body was strong as he held her, feeling her forehead pressed warmly against the roughness of his unshaven cheek. He could feel her breathe, the impossibly strong, warm body of the woman he had unconsciously loved from a distance now molding into his, whatever separateness which once might have existed between them now suddenly becoming indistinguishable. Then, wanting to see how she also felt, he looked at her and saw the warm, powerful depth of her eyes also glistening in the sparse light of the room.

∞

It was a warmer night than it had been for weeks, though the air remained crisp, soldiers and others still dressing warmly as they made their way to the outskirts of the base. A phonograph had been set up, playing a record of a famous Parisian chanteuse singing poignantly about lost love, the meaning of which was lost on no one among the group of men and women whose only thought was of home. Another grouping of soldiers who had not given in to melancholy sat laughing and drinking, while others danced with the nurses dressed in their long skirts and aprons, who, despite regulations to the contrary, humored them out of loyalty as though reminding themselves what they were fighting for. And the soldiers responded in kind, each thankful to be holding a woman in his arms.

Burke and Forsythe sat and watched soldiers and army personnel laughing and carrying on, despite the war which continued only miles away. Harrold studied some of the soldiers, realizing for himself that he had become more jaded with time. Both Harrold and Burke had read the reports coming off of the wire, seeing that what had been true before—that battles and varying missions had been glorified and filled with hyperbole—was now even more true, and with a vengeance. But the reality had remained the same. The horror of men being shattered by battle, the thousands battered and beaten, some driven insane by the sheer brutality of life at the front, could not be assuaged by any semblance of manipulative headlines or the sanitized accounts that found their way home. Instead, it left those who had experienced engagement walking around like ghosts, staring into the distance with the pain and fear of terrorized men forced to live the rest of their lives in ravaged and broken bodies.

Burke poured Harrold a glass of whisky, smirking to himself at the fully inebriated Englishman. Harrold paused, absently directing his commentary in the Irishman's direction.

"So where the hell is that woman of yours?"

"She had to go to the train depot in Amiens to pick up more supplies. She'll be coming in on the next transport."

Harrold snickered drunkenly despite himself, knowing by now such a comment was meant more as a euphemism for what she was acquiring for the RAMC using the oldest of war-depleted devices—cold, hard cash proffered to the increasingly mercenary types infiltrating the black market.

"It could be dangerous, you know. I'm surprised you didn't go with her."

Burke smiled wryly. "Of anyone I know, she can take care of herself."

Harrold shook his head as he continued to watch the women and their beaux dancing by. In contrast to his own dour mood, they seemed filled with life, as though realizing that they might actually make it back to their homes and families alive. Rawlinson's Fourth Army had just hit the German forces hard outside the plateau near Amiens, supported by the French First and Third Armies, and the Thirty-third Illinois Division under the British III Corps. Four hundred tanks, two hundred single-engine aircraft and nine Allied divisions went up against Marwitz's Second Army, their ultimate sights set on regaining the ground lost during the last German offensive. The attack had begun at 04:20 with battalions of soldiers arranged in five waves which moved forward in a creeping barrage, motion which had been obscured by a heavy fog. With the smell of smoke and gasoline filling the air, the Germans, already suffering losses, had been soundly defeated.

It was with this victory that for the first time the base had allowed the soldiers to openly celebrate what would later be dubbed the "Black Day of the German Army," as troops of men drank, sang songs by Gilbert and Sullivan and staged bawdy theatricals on a quickly constructed dais toward the middle of the camp. Others flirted with nurses by the light of several bonfires, while what rare cattle and hogs were requisitioned from local farms, braised on several spits. The soldiers laughed, drank and ate heartily, celebrating letting their hair down for the first time in months.

Maeve soon arrived. She walked up to them and stood quietly just as Burke finished his drink. She was dressed in her normal uniform, the sleeves of her shirt rolled up to her elbows, though this time her hair was down and loose over her shoulders. She reached down and poured whisky into a nearby glass which had been left empty.

Harrold felt her behind him, watching the scene that had managed to hold his fascination. "We were just wondering when the hell you'd get here."

"Some of us work for a living, Harrold, but believe me, I wasn't about to let you have all the fun." She looked around, watching the men and women dancing. She shook her head. "You'd think there wasn't a war on."

Burke turned to her and asked quietly. "Get your supplies?"

She took a swig from the drink Burke handed to her, nodding. "They're even more expensive now than at the beginning. They probably know they won't have much more time to run their racket."

"Will you have any money left?"

She smiled. "Enough."

Harrold again chortled drunkenly, choosing to ignore them, instead still fixated on the fraternization continuing blatantly before them. "I wonder how many of these women will be pregnant next month— or men in need treatment for some goddamned disease they picked up from one of the whorehouses in Paris." He turned to Maeve, seeing her amused expression, as though chiding him for his drunken diatribe. "Well, God knows now how many, including that one surgeon among you lot, have picked up some kind of plague. Between Sailly la Bourse and Montmartre, the Germans could win from the clap alone, though theirs is no doubt as bloody bad as ours. That and whatever else is circulating these days."

Maeve smiled as she watched them dance. "And I suppose you won't be one of those poor bastards, needing to come to me after such unmitigated depravity."

"A contingent of whores, my dear doctor, is not my idea of a good time. I'd rather bide my time among more rarefied company."

"Such as?" Burke asked, amused.

Maeve laughed heartily, shaking her head at the thought. Young debutantes from Nairobi, newly come out, and ripe for the picking. Though she had heard much worse, and had seen it more times than she wanted to remember, often needing to treat soldiers for more than their trench-line injuries. For months, she had barely had enough Salvarsan, and even before that, mercury and whatever iodides she could find in treating syphilis. The longer the men were on the front, the more illnesses would become rampant, including any number of ailments which had nothing to do with combat. Whatever escape could be had would be utilized to make men forget they may as well have been in purgatory before, in transport to the line, they were consigned to a living hell.

Harrold stared at same scene she did, causing him to shake his head—a few hundred men being in the immediate vicinity, replacing those that had been there the week before, with more to appear weeks later as, despite further Allied victory, the carnage continued. He turned to Maeve. "So where's your patriotism, O'Hanlon? Aren't you anxious to go home and procreate just so we'll have another generation to send off when another war comes? And it will. Peace isn't peace anymore. It's a long, drawn-out cease fire."

"Indeed, and among the grandchildren of Victoria, if I'm not mistaken." She smiled, choosing her words with the intent to irritate him. "Was it any wonder we Yanks overthrew you— considering wars in Europe always seem to result from empires squabbling over who has what territory thousands of miles away. And we'll see what else is carved up after this is over."

He shook his head again, his voice slurred. "As

though you have anything to say about it, dear girl. You may be in British uniform, but you're an American, and your government has made a bloody fortune even before sending your own boys off to be slaughtered. Come in late to the war, not to mention cornering the market on the bloody goddamned profits." He chortled to himself. "So, what will happen...Britain will win more territory, Germany will lose whatever to which it feels most entitled, and we will go on with our bloody celebrations over gins and tonic, as though nothing ever happened. But it still won't be over. And you'll have more bodies to work on next time 'round—whether here or some other God-forsaken part of the world."

Burke watched as Harrold poured another shot, motioning absently to her. "Frankly, I'm amazed the RAMC even allowed you here at all, much less as a surgeon." He then shook his head. "Should have been the bloody Women's Hospital Corps—at least the nurses there are comforting and look pretty—they give the men something to concentrate on instead of their pain. And giving you a rank of captain of all things..."

Maeve smiled wryly. "Perhaps you think they'd be better off without me."

Harrold turned, staring at her. "Perhaps they would at that. Then you'd be home safe instead of here."

Maeve bowed her head, remaining silent. Burke looked at her, after a moment placing his hand on her shoulder. She turned to him and he nodded toward where others were dancing as though to get away. She stood, taking his hand for a turn on the dance floor. They moved to the outer edge where no one stood as Burke put his arms around her, leading her gently in a waltz several feet away.

Maeve smirked at him, her tone pleasantly sarcastic. "I keep forgetting you can't dance worth a damn."

"That's the whisky talking. Or you're letting him get to you."

"I'm as much a Celt as you are. Sometimes

melancholy just seeps out whether the whisky's available or not."

He smiled. "It's not easy for an Englishman to admit he's smitten."

She chuckled. "He has an odd way of showing it." Maeve shook her head, smiling slightly. She turned toward Harrold, watching him arguing politics with several soldiers. "I imagine, though, when all of this is over, he'll wish he were back at Muthaiga."

"He'd want to be anywhere as long as it's not London." He then turned, looking at the soldiers dancing with nurses around them. "Not like the men here."

Maeve nodded. "Perhaps someday they'll find what we both have. You've been here long enough, you forget you have a life anywhere else. And you don't want to even think about what it will be like to go home." She closed her eyes, her body suddenly becoming cold, as she trembled in the night air, deriving comfort from the warmth of his body. "I never thought there would be a day when I'd be afraid of what would happen when the war was over…or how I would live the rest of my life." She looked at him, her jaw tensing, and if he hadn't known her better, showing a fear unlike her. But her voice was warm, as was the expression in her eyes. "Burke, what have we done?"

Burke looked into her eyes, not allowing her to see anything else but the honesty of his expression, his deep voice suddenly firm. "What we were meant to do. With no regrets."

Burke and Harrold walked slowly, the Englishman shuffling forward, leaning hard on Burke, as he sang Gilbert and Sullivan off-key. Burke tried to tune him out as he moved Harrold through the camp until they found their way to the tent, suffering the glances of several other reporters who were also stumbling in. Maeve had already gone back to her barracks, having saved the Englishman from the ANZAC contingent, each of whom were more than happy for the discussion to come to blows if it had progressed much further, the thought of cold-cocking a colonel, and better yet a high-handed British colonial among their ranks, not offering too much displeasure. Harrold had escaped, ignoring the fact that Maeve had saved him from sure embarrassment. It had been enough just to hear her voice, feeling the warmth that shone in her eyes as, amused, she led him surreptitiously away.

Burke opened the door to the room, watching Harrold collapse drunkenly on his bed, his eyes closed as he landed hard on the thin mattress.

"Bastards…" Harrold whispered. "Christ—you'd think there'd be someone left with a goddamned sense of humor." He raised his head. "You don't think she hates me, do you?"

Burke didn't answer as Harrold groaned.

"I couldn't bear it if she did. She's the kind of woman I should have married if I had known there was such a thing—or had a choice." Harrold looked at him quietly for a moment and leaned forward, his voice suddenly serious, as he stared at the Irishman earnestly, making sure Burke took note. "She's the best thing that has happened to you, you dour Irish bastard—hopefully you know what you've got."

Burke watched with wry amusement as Harrold fell back against the cot. Harrold laughed bitterly, his eyes becoming heavy. He stared at the Celt a few more moments. "Be sure to give her my love, Reginald," he whispered. "…before you forget to give her yours."

Within moments, Harrold dropped off to sleep. Burke left the still empty barracks, closing the flap behind him as he wandered back to Maeve's tent.

He arrived a few minutes later, opening the flap, and found Maeve asleep. He moved over to her silently, sitting down on the chair. He touched her hair, caressing it the soft, dark blonde waves underneath his fingers as he stroked them gently. He then moved slowly, so as not to wake her, crawling into the cot, his chest against the breadth of her back, reaching gently around her waist to hold her. She didn't stir, and within moments, comforted by the warmth of her body, he went to sleep with her in his arms.

It was relatively silent outside, the sun not yet rising over the horizon when Burke felt her move. He had awakened before dawn, as he did most mornings, watching her, for some reason having reveled in the strange serenity he had found as she slept. She opened her eyes, looking at him, seeing the strength in his rough countenance, the strong features and the lines which had been carved over the years into his face, both from war and whatever it was that had come before it. She smiled gently, settling back into him. He softened as she spoke, her voice a whisper. "How long have you been awake?"

"A while. I wanted to watch you sleep."

He reached brushed the hair from her forehead, feeling the softness of her skin as he kissed her temple gently. She looked at him, smiling at the strangely gentle expression on his face. She then looked down, touching a scar on the upper part of his chest.

"Where did you get this?"

"Old country. Several years ago."

She remained silent, watching a memory flit across his face.

"My parents moved us from Ireland when I was fourteen. We had lived near Lahinch, near the Cliffs of Moher. I used to dream about it—the waves crashing against black rock, the cliffs dropping sharply into the sea." He paused, looking at her. "I came back several years later, when things started heating up."

She smiled knowingly. "And you got involved."

He nodded. "I was covering the north—Armagh to Belfast. The Nationalists got into a fight with several

Ulstermen outside of a Protestant church in Derry. A British police officer thought I was just another Mick bastard ready to take down a British soldier, even though I didn't have a gun in my hand." He paused. "When the war started, the BEF started enlisting Irish for the Tenth—the papers began telling tales of Germans raping nuns and that zeppelins would soon be crossing the channel. I was already here on my own reporting for the wire when Redmond went to Parliament to recruit nationalists for the Sixteenth. Once they found out who I was, it was decided it would be better to have me cover the front instead of fighting on it. They'd rather have Nationalists in their army fighting a common enemy even while back home riots and rebellions are going on."

She smiled. "And after all that you've been able to tolerate Harrold."

Burke laughed. "He's shown he can report on more than the perfect gin and tonic."

"It's not the first time you've befriended an English soldier, even though we're all on the same side, whether people remember it after all this or not."

Burke looked at her questioningly.

She raised her eyebrow, a small, sad smile at her lips, as though she'd always known more than she had let on. "I've heard the stories...Germans crossing no-man's-land, slaughtering BEF and ANZAC already down on the field. You shot four, including the sergeant leading the advance. It's one of the reasons soldiers trust you."

He frowned at her. "How did you know?"

Maeve smiled gently. "One of the surgeons operated on the men you saved. We heard about it when you first came here."

She bowed her head. "Within a few weeks of first coming to the line, a group of us was sent to Verdun. The French army had a shortage of doctors, maybe one or two surgeons to cover several clearing stations down the line. The RAMC sent reinforcements until the French could bring in several more medical staff from Paris and the colonies. When we got there, the whole base hospital was filled with bodies. The stench was so strong we could barely breathe. We tried to save the soldiers who were still alive, but there was nothing—no morphine, styptics, nothing...we even ended up having to transfuse several of the soldiers we thought might live with our own blood. By the time I got back to barracks, my hands were shaking. They didn't stop shaking for weeks. The older medical staff wanted nothing of it—they had all pulled rank for duty back in rest stations in Paris. Maybe one of the reasons we were able to save the ones we did was because we were young, just out of school and willing to try anything." She shook her head. "To this day I would have thought I'd have a hard time being here. But I found most of the surgeons here didn't give a damn who I was— just as long as I could hold my own. I even took on the cases they wouldn't, at first because of stubbornness and something to prove, but later because I couldn't stand seeing another soldier die when there was something I could do to save him, no matter the personal cost. You never knew who might be waiting for him, even if he didn't have family. Life was precious. At that point, nothing else was important. All you wanted was to see them live long enough to go home."

Burke watched as Maeve moved from his arms and stood, a strange expression on her face as she walked over to the flap of the tent. She lifted it, inviting the coolness of the air on her skin which rose in gooseflesh within moments, the soft haze of sunlight shining through. She looked out silently, her body in silhouette, a soft halo of light around her as she stared down into the heart of the camp. "They're going back tomorrow...even though command thinks the war will soon be over."

"They'll push even harder now to demoralize the Germans."

She paused, watching several soldiers head toward Sunday Mass. After a few moments, Burke stood, moving behind her. She breathed deeply in the damp air, dew on the ground. She watched the priest welcoming the soldiers to services which amounted to several chairs and a portable altar. The priest began services and her eyes glistened as she heard the first words of the Catholic liturgy. She turned to him, smiling wanly. "When I was a little girl, my father used to take me to Mass and made me promise never to tell my mother. He would pray in Latin, speak to the priest in Irish…He even taught me a prayer he made me promise to remember. That was the prayer I said when he died."

He watched as she moved over to her collection of books. She picked one out, handing it to him. He opened it and discovered an antique rosary inside.

"My father gave it to me when I was a girl. It had been his grandmother's. They're the only things I brought with me from the States."

Burke looked at her, his eyes glistening.

"You never noticed, but the book you gave me was the same one my father gave to me when he died."

Burke turned the pages, recognizing the same passage he had once marked for her.

> *I dteas na hansachta má táim ag lonrahm*
> *Duitse thar aon ghrá dá dtaibhsíonn ar domhan duit*
> *I slí is go bhfaighim cloíte cumhacht do shúl leis*
> *Ó radharc thar barr atá le foghlaim oilte*
> *Chun siúl ar aghaidh I slí na maithe d'fhoghlaim.*
> *Is maith a chím mar tá t'intlíochtsa tuilte*
> *Den niamh a lasas inti ón solas síoraí*
> *A adhnas I gcónaí grá gan ach é a d'fheiscint…*

"The night I first saw you, I remember opening to this page," she said quietly. "I felt as though someone were standing there, for whatever reason making sure it was the first thing I'd see." She shook her head. "A man writing about heaven and hell, somehow transcending the world in which he found himself. All of these years, and in the moment you never realize might come, you suddenly remember what it means to be alive," she said quietly. "Until you, my father was the only human being I ever really loved. I've lived my life to make him proud. To be what he wanted, even though it never made sense to anyone else. I became what he never could be, only later realizing perhaps he lived his life as he did so I could be here, doing what I'm doing now. And more than that, in these last months, I've also come to believe every one of those moments led to these, as though some part of him knew I would also come here, both to do what I've done, but also so I could find you." She looked at him quietly. "There isn't a day which goes by when I am not thankful to have you in my life. My life never made sense until I came here, being among these men, doing what I could to heal them. But I didn't remember my soul until you." She paused, her tone then changing. "Loving you, now I know why men pray. It's as though whatever God exists means us to know what this feels like." She shook her head, hesitant. "We've never talked about whether or not you believe in God. But if anything ever happens, I want you to promise me something. I said a prayer for my father when he died— promise me that you'd say a prayer for me."

He frowned. "Nothing is going to happen."

"Maybe not. But promise me."

He stared at her silently. She frowned, dropping her gaze to the floor.

"I'm going to the line again in a few days."

She nodded, knowing then that he would not answer her. "I know."

Several hours later the camp bustled with activity. Horses and lorries moved by, kicking up dust in their wake as they headed east along the Somme, ready to continue the push toward the Belgian border to the south having already pushed past the long-held German salient near Chateau-

Thierry at La Rocq plateau. Maeve stood with Burke, watching him pack his gear. She bowed her head, her jaw tightening. He noticed and smiled gently.

"I'll be back tomorrow. And—Harrold will be here. They won't let him out of here having reopened that infamous wound of his."

She nodded. "Maybe I'll go comfort him while you're away. We'll just stay away from discussing anything serious."

She raised her eyebrows with gentle amusement as he moved over to her, kissing her. She pulled away, looking into his eyes. "I'll see you when you get back."

He nodded, stroking her neck with the back of his fingers, then reaching to do the same with her cheek. She smiled and watched as he stepped away, slinging his backpack over his shoulder. Maeve watched him leave, meeting the rest of the small corps of journalists standing by the military transport nearby.

She continued watching him from a distance, seeing him shaking hands with a couple of the men, waiting with them as the rest piled onto the transport with a company of soldiers.

Maeve stared forward, her voice soft as she watched him enter the vehicle, the transport beginning to pull away. "*Tá grá agam dhuit*," she whispered. "I love you."

Burke sat among the soldiers as the transport moved along the bumpy road toward the line outside of Amiens. The men were mostly silent, many lost in their thoughts as others smoked or talked quietly while watching the passing scenery. Burke studied them. He could hear mortars in the distance as he looked down the line of men, the rifles at their sides like another appendage.

It was then that he saw one of the Irish soldiers

formerly in a regiment of the Sixteenth Irish Division who had been amalgamated into the Fourth Army, unaware anyone was watching him. He was young, not more than eighteen years old. His eyes were averted, his head bowed to stare at the glass beads of a rosary which he gripped tightly in his hands. After a moment, Burke realized that he had been praying. The boy crossed himself, finishing his prayer.

"*An paidrín.*"

The soldier looked up, hearing Burke's voice. He stared at the older man silently for a moment, then nodded.

"*Cad is ainm duit?*"

"*Thomas Halloran. Cad fútsa?*"

"Reginald Burke." Burke smiled kindly, seeing the tension leave the boy's face from Burke's gentle words in his own language. "*Tá áthas orm bualadh leat.*"

The boy nodded then bowed his head once again, fear moving through him, as he watched the road, the front lines looming in the distance.

Maeve grabbed a bandage and tore open the packaging, checking Harrold's dressing before staring at him with mock annoyance that she had to deal with the same wound as before.

"So, you've recovered from last night?"

Maeve smiled knowingly. "I should ask you the same thing." She paused, taking off his old bandage, seeing the oozing, stitched wound, not yet having begun to heal. "Jesus, Harrold—what have you been doing to this thing?"

"I've never been what you call a fast healer. It didn't help that the place nearly turned into a brawl before we left."

She clipped the bandage away, running a damp cloth over it. Harrold winced visibly, sucking in his breath.

"Hold still, Forsythe, otherwise this is going to hurt." She smiled, readying the new bandage. "You keep going like this, you won't be writing for a while."

"As though that were a disappointment." He laughed again, this time to himself. "It's a necessary evil—going out into the trenches, reporting on rats and rotting corpses," he said. "To tell you the truth, I'd be happy never to write again."

She looked at him questioningly.

"Gladys wrote to me. It seems I'll be going into the family business when I return. The sometime literary home of aristocrats who seek to publish their memoirs about how their nannies seduced them at the age of fourteen." He turned to Maeve, seeing her amused expression. "The family thought I should have gotten into publishing in the first place instead of attempting to bore the world with any misguided attempts at journalism." He snorted. "But it's also family tradition for a man to have his stint in Nairobi before coming home…even should the world itself and all of its infernal reality happen in the meantime."

Maeve smiled and continued tying his bandage. "Well, I'd imagine working with writers would suit you. And I can't imagine you would miss all of this."

He shook his head. "No, they're right. I'm not cut out for it. Reporters for the most part are highly romanticized lunatics, if you want to know the truth."

She laughed. "How do you mean?"

"Like that man you're in love with. He's the real writer among us all."

She smiled, his bluntness not surprising her. "So I'm in love with a lunatic."

"Yes, but I think you know that already." He shook his head, testing out the bandage, extending his arm. "He's changed, you know."

She looked at him, tossing his old bandages into the overflowing can of refuse which had remained since that morning, and which Harrold had summarily ignored.

"If I were to hazard a guess, I'd say that he's almost content, if you could even call it that. Not that you can easily tell, considering he scowls most of the time, figuring the rest of us are all complete sods. You're the exception, of course. He doesn't say much and the rest he saves for print. God help the lot of us if someday he has nothing to write about."

A medic suddenly rushed in, as the sound of sirens began, shattering the relative quiet of the camp. He paused sheepishly, seeing her cleaning up, Harrold still sitting before her. "I'm sorry to disturb you, Ma'am, but we have incoming wounded."

"How bad?"

"White star and yellow cross shells, Ma'am. Phosgene and mustard gas—hit an entire company."

She nodded. "I'm finished. I'll be right there."

The medic then ducked out. She turned to Harrold, grinning at him knowingly. "So—you want to stay here, or head outside?"

"Well if you remember, I'm not completely fond of surgical needles. I'll stay."

She smiled, nodding, as she headed for the door, placing her hand as the warm gesture of a friend on his other shoulder as she left the room.

Maeve climbed inside the ambulance and examined one of the patients, the other having already died in transit. The soldier who was still alive stared at her wildly, his body shaking in shock. The nurse beside Maeve looked over to her, assisting her in pulling back the soldier's breeches.

"There it is."

The soldier noticed her surgeon's clothing. He stared at her harshly, icy eyes peering from his blood-stained face, his gaze blank, almost hollow. The nurse moved in to take over, but Maeve shook her head briefly, stopping her. The nurse paused, her eyes widening as she saw the man's expression.

"I'm going to try to save your life if you'll let me

take a look at you," Maeve said gently. She then paused, knowing that if she didn't continue to look solidly into his eyes he might react violently to any sudden movement like a cornered animal.

"Ma'am, let me fetch one of the other doctors—"

Maeve shook her head, still not taking her eyes from the soldier's, seeing that he was about to snap. "No... Just go and get some gauze for his wound, please..."

The nurse paused, uneasy. "You sure, Ma'am?"

Maeve nodded.

As she did, the soldier grabbed her viciously by the wrist, twisting it violently. Maeve stifled herself from letting out a cry as she could feel the tension in his hand, as though in a single movement, and despite her own strength, the bone would break. Amidst the pain she steadied herself, seeing the insanity and fury of acute shell shock blazing in his eyes. The soldier paused, his voice coming out in a sharp hiss, his eyes wide. "*They're coming...*" He then backed from her, his body beginning to shudder violently as he went further into shock. One of the nurses grabbed the cloth soaked with ether and placed it over his mouth from behind, watching as he slowly lost consciousness, his body being taken away quickly toward the surgical tent. She then turned to Maeve, who was holding her wrist tightly. "You all right, Ma'am?"

Maeve nodded, motioning to the operating theater nearby, shaking off the pain. She then spoke, her voice low. "Put him on a table and get him ready for surgery. If another doctor isn't there, let me know and I'll take care of him." She shuddered, pausing to lean against a gurney to catch her breath as the nurse and stretcher bearer took the soldier inside.

Harrold watched as she moved from the ambulance, the drivers carrying the soldier toward surgery. He approached her, seeing her rubbing the skin around her wrist, still dazed.

"Are you all right?"

Maeve nodded.

"You did what you could."

Maeve smiled wanly, nodding.

After several minutes she was then sitting beside him on the ground of the tent in his and Burke's barracks. Harrold handed her a flask, which she looked at for a moment before refusing.

"He had been at Mons in 1914, during the first engagement with the Germans."

"No wonder he's insane," Harrold said gently. "You remember what they apparently saw."

She shook her head at his response, as though she would have expected it. "They always say that the end of a war is when there are the most casualties...that he will be lucky to get shipped back. All the while everyone praying that their number won't be up just before they're about to go home...." She paused, looking at Harrold quietly. "They'll operate on him and then take him to a rest hospital in London. If he's lucky, he'll go to the country for a rest cure...if he's not, they'll fill him with enough electric current to power an entire hospital wing." She shook her head. "It's an abomination what they do to men who have already been through hell. You'd think they'd give them whatever peace they can."

"Maybe they think they are. He did a pretty good job on your wrist."

She looked down at the bruising that had begun on her skin. She rubbed it absently and smiled. "I'll survive." She then paused, her voice more serious. "Tell me about something else. Tell me what he's doing right now. Burke."

Harrold looked at her, thinking for a moment. "He's probably with the soldiers, listening to their stories. From what I understand, he's escaped death more times than anyone can count—and always attributes it to luck." He paused again for a moment, shaking his head with amusement. "He won't admit it, perhaps, but he'd be lost without war. When it's over, he'll have to find something else to replace it, or else find another battlefield somewhere where people are killing each another..." Harrold said gently. "Maybe it's the writing that saves him. Lambasting the world for its ills has to be pretty bloody therapeutic." He smiled. "But it suits him— whether or not we all deserve it. He's an angry man whose fury comes out like the harshest poetry. But I also think you're the only one who has ever truly made him happy."

Maeve bowed her head, pausing for a moment before she again began speaking, her voice changing, almost halting, a strange expression on her face as though the last hours' events had taken more of a toll than she had let on. Harrold frowned, trying to read her face. "Before heading to the front, I went to Notre Dame in Paris. There was a woman there, saying a prayer for her husband. We were there, sitting before the stations of the cross. She was lighting a candle and pointed to one beside hers. I didn't know why I was lighting it at the time. It was as though she knew what I was thinking. She turned from me and looked up at the candle she had just lit and said that one day I'd look into another's eyes—husband or child—and I would never be the same—that loving another human being is truly the closest thing to knowing God."

Harrold paused, bowing his head as he listened, hearing the softness of her voice.

"All this time, all of the people in my life whom I've loved, even the men I've been able to save, I never knew what she meant. I never even really knew if I believed in anything at all, at least, not the 'God' you're always taught to believe in, my mother and father always being at opposite ends of the spectrum—Catholic and Protestant at war in their own home. I respected my father's belief, while my mother's was a farce—just another way to *disapprove* of others under the guise of some judgmental creed she herself barely understood. I never understood any of it until realizing their marriage was about her status and his money, even if she did love him once upon a time. It just was what it was—and after a while, no love between them."

She smiled, knowing the import of her words on Harrold, given his own life, and what he would go back to.

"Now the only thing I know is that what this one woman said, in Notre Dame, made the only sense I've ever felt. At the time I figured it was true because of a daughter's love for her father, but now—"

Harrold stared at her gently. "And now?"

Maeve looked at him quietly. "Knowing Burke."

It was an hour or more before dawn as Maeve stirred, having fallen asleep against Harrold, whose arms were still gently around her, his head cocked back against the side of the tent. She gently moved from him, standing to move over to the flap of the tent, looking outside. The camp was silent except for a steady rain which had begun to fall as dawn approached. The nurses had known where she was and had apparently left her, believing that she needed the sleep, and knowing that she was safe.

As she looked toward the edge of the camp, a chill ran through her as she listened to the stillness. There was something wrong. It was only moments later that she realized what was making her uneasy, as she saw a series of shadows fall across the canvas of one of the tents nearby.

Harrold awakened groggily, feeling her move, seeing her come to stand at the flap of the tent and hearing the same, punctuated stillness. He breathed deeply, his faculties suddenly sharpening, the few instincts he had acquired from the line now kicking in enough to feel what she did, however differently. He paused, feeling his own surge of adrenaline as he watched her stand slowly less than a foot away.

Harrold knew then what must have occurred to her, as it had to him the moment he felt the silence. For the last week, there had been reports of looting and scouting parties of German and Austro-Hungarian soldiers retreating across the front, taking what they could while slipping past Allied forces toward the Ardennes, where they would then return back unnoticed into their own territory. With the war nearly at an end, and feelers having been sent out regarding an Armistice, battle-worn, some half-mad and violent, certain among them had killed several soldiers and camp personnel in their retreat, hitting the periphery of camps or sections along the line hoping to find either usable munitions or provisions, then slipping away and gaining enough ground to outdistance anyone among varying sections who might have been after them. Most had already retreated past the Somme, but there had been reports of others who had been waiting out the retreat. It was the danger of war believed to be won, so that the forces could not afford to let down their guard. But in many instances, they had, and it now appeared that their camp was one of those which had left a gap in whatever security, by sheer proximity to the line, should have been assured.

Maeve could feel the uneasiness nagging at her when she saw shadows moving across the ground, knowing that they were not British soldiers. She couldn't tell from the shape of their clothing, but there was something distinctly wrong about the shadows' movement. Worse still, their location was on the periphery of the camp, several hundred yards away from post command, any of the other bivouacs gone or other barracks empty from soldiers who had been sent to the line the day before, those whom they had replaced not yet having returned. The clearing station was also silent, as the nurses and surgeons were the only ones who would have been in earshot. But they also were what the scouting party would be looking for, attempting to take whatever food, medical supplies and morphine they might need, both to help them keep going, or to knock themselves into oblivion. For all intents and purposes, unless they moved now, they would be unheard should she and

Harrold be found.

She turned, looking around the room. Harrold stood, moving to the doorway, again having heard what she did. He looked outside. Maeve stared at him, her expression frozen. Harrold backed up, his head arched backward as the barrel of a pistol moved inches away from his head. A soldier entered the tent, his face and body dirty, the remnants of a German dragoon uniform soaked with rain on his tall frame, water dripping from his face. The German stared at Harrold, whispering behind him. Maeve's expression hardened, understanding enough of his words to realize they would be killed if they didn't cooperate. The German turned around as two more soldiers ambled inside. Maeve breathed, remaining still, as the soldiers approached Harrold, backing him up against the wall.

The first German barked orders to the men with him, and then he turned, peering at Maeve for several moments in silence. He then spoke to her in German. "*Englisch?*" No reaction. "*Amerikanisch?*"

Maeve remained silent, refusing to speak. He turned, in a harsh whisper barking an order to one of the other soldiers. A soldier placed his pistol directly against Harrold's head. Maeve trembled, now hearing the sound of thunder in the distance. There was no chance now that they would be heard, even if one of them fired.

The soldier cocked the gun and stared at her, the sound of thunder cracking behind him. Satisfied by the noise which would silence any move he made, he moved the barrel slightly, toying with the man at the other end. Harrold moved slightly, and within moments, the movement alone caused the soldier's gun to twitch, and then, as though irritated by the colonial's audacity, he shot Harrold in the chest, blood flowing from the wound and showering the room within a short radius from where he fell. Maeve tried to go to him, but the dragoon stopped her, grabbing her forcefully by the throat. He frowned, closing his fingers tighter, his voice slurred. He then struck her, sending her sprawling onto the floor.

"*Fracht ist das Vakuum? Äther....Morphium?*"

She shook her head. The German then took the pistol from the soldier who had shot Harrold, and staring into her eyes, pointed the gun at her. "*Hängenden Schwein...*"

Harrold watched, now bloodied on the floor, as the German pulled the trigger. He closed his eyes, hearing the sound of the gunshot hitting flesh. He then opened his eyes, seeing Maeve before him. Her chest had exploded, her body slammed forcefully to the ground. Maeve's skin paled as she tried to move, backing weakly away, her senses fading slowly from consciousness as she felt herself hit the wall behind them, pain coursing through her until she could barely breathe.

The German, unmoved by her state, lowered himself drunkenly to the ground, taking a pocketknife from his jacket pocket, placing the point at the waist of her breeches. Maeve stared at the officer, her voice harsh, coming through clenched teeth. She was losing consciousness, her skin paling as the blood continued draining from her body. She stared at him, even in her pain, her gray eyes flashing.

"*Si vous me violer, vous pouvez aussi bien me tuer...*"

The German looked over to one of the others, who translated. The German laughed and turned back to her, wrenching her legs apart. Harrold watched, his body crumpled against the wall. Had she been able to make a sound, he could not hear it, as he watched the German cover her mouth, whispering to her harshly in words Harrold could not hear. He then slit the material of her breeches, tearing them from her body. Maeve opened her eyes, which were now glistening, watching him fumble for his belt. Positioning himself, he entered her, thrusting brutally. Her body shuddered, her eyes staring forward, as though she knew what was coming. A moment later, in a single, slow movement, he slit her throat.

There was no sound. Harrold could feel the bile rising in his throat, and he began coughing as he watched Maeve's head dropping against the ground, her eyes staring forward, the pool of blood spreading slowly across the floor. The German thrust several more times into her motionless body until satisfied, removing himself from her, his movements rough as he then barked at the other soldiers, closing his trousers. The other soldiers withdrew, drunken and dazed as they made their way unseen from the tent. Still pointing the bloody knife at Harrold, the remaining officer chortled to himself, stains from fresh blood covering the front of his uniform as he disappeared with his men outside the door.

Harrold turned to Maeve. Her head was cocked awkwardly against the floor, her last moments gone, her suddenly lifeless eyes glistening as she stared out into space.

Forty miles away, a corps of Allied soldiers moved slowly to the east of the Somme, feeling the aftermath of the onslaught of mortars and bullets which had started at dawn. The haze of fog and the smoke from fire drifted over the ground, making it difficult to see. Soldiers covered the field, a few stray shots of gunfire heard in the distance. In the background, an officer called blindly into the fog, announcing the enemy's retreat.

Burke walked slowly among the dead bodies of Allied soldiers. He came to stop before one of them, kneeling down. He bowed his head, recognizing the young boy's face as the one with whom he rode to the front, seeing the boy's bloodied uniform, his body half blown away. Beside him he saw a glint coming from the weak rays of sunlight shining through the trees. He reached down, feeling the hardness of dark beads underneath his fingers. He looked down, the boy's rosary lying loosely in the dirt. Burke took it slowly, holding it tightly in his hands.

∞

The sirens had sounded for several hours, screaming in rapid succession. Several lorries pulled up, medics and soldiers getting out, as doctors and nurses ran to meet them. A strange pall had fallen over the camp, which Burke noticed as he descended from the transport, slinging his pack over his shoulder.

He stood, peering curiously toward the clearing station as a soldier walked up to him. The soldier pointed to one of the surgical units where patients rested following surgery. Burke stared, his expression suddenly deadened of emotion as he followed the younger man toward the surgical tent.

Burke walked inside the door, nodding to one of the nurses, who peered at him sheepishly, not looking him in the eye. Burke then looked across the room, seeing Harrold on one of the hospital beds. He walked over to him, lighting his usual cigarette, though this time he used it as a shield to hide his face as the smoke wafted up toward the ceiling. One of the nurses stared at him, thinking better of saying anything. Then seeing who he was, she excused herself hurriedly from the room. Burke cleared his throat.

"Harrold…"

Harrold turned and looked into his friend's eyes, his own bloodshot, as he watched Burke sit and put his head in his hands.

Harrold turned away, his body shaking, pain shooting through him more from seeing Burke's face than from his own wounds. Burke bowed his head, gently pulling back the sheets. He paused, seeing the extensive bandages on Harrold's right side, below his collarbone where the bullet entered his body.

"Three Germans were caught by the Americans raiding another camp near Baupame," he said quietly. "They were shot trying to escape."

Harrold turned suddenly, staring at him.

"She told them to kill her, didn't she?"

Harrold paused, for a moment unable to speak, and then bleating out the only response he could think of. "How did you know?"

Burke's jaw set, the emotion coursing through him which made him also barely get the words out. "It's what I would have done."

Harrold then collapsed, hard, masculine sobs racking through his body. Burke placed his hand on the Englishman's shoulder. His expression had fallen, devoid of any emotion he couldn't control. But his emotions would soon get the better of him, enough so that he stood and left Harrold alone in the small area corded off from the rest of the surgical unit.

Burke walked outside, hearing the last of the transports moving in, the camp finally quieting for the night. He stared into the sky, seeing the clouds that had rolled in over the last few hours, thunder still breaking in the distance. No one was around him as a sob rose in his throat, which he pushed away, heading to his quarters so as not to be seen.

The light from the single flame was visible from the floor, where Burke sat with a bottle of whiskey, an oil lamp beside him. Maeve lay beside him, uncovered on a wooden slab, her eyes closed. Her hair was down, streaming across her shoulders, her face ghostly, her lips colorless. He looked at her quietly. After a moment, he touched her, running his fingers across the line of her jaw, feeling the softness of her skin. The wound on her neck had been sutured tightly, her chest wound closed and hidden by a rough wool blanket placed gently over her body.

Pain moved through him as he looked at her, feeling the stale stillness in the room, the chemical and salty smell of iodine hanging, causing his stomach to turn. He bowed his head. His movements were slow, awkward, having nearly finished his bottle enough to fumble, knocking it over, the last of its contents spilling out onto the floor. He raised the bottle quickly, correcting it, as he did so, feeling the emotion flood over him that he had been holding back since his arrival in the camp. He looked at her, tears now in his eyes.

"Maeve..."

He was drunk, his words slurred. He paused for several moments, trembling. He then took her hand in his, finding it cold, lifeless. He touched her fingers and the smoothness of her skin, the strength of bone and sinew in a surgeon's hands. His voice broke as he started at her, her name coming out in a whisper.

"Maeve..."

Burke entered Maeve's barracks, surveying the room. Everything had remained untouched, her cot unmade, the covers rumpled and pulled back from where she had slept. Volumes of books sat on her nightstand, along with her few belongings.

Burke moved over to the stand, touching the objects on it softly. Among them was her copy of *An Choimeide Dhiaga*, the book he had given to her. He picked it up, seeing that she had continued to keep the page marked. He opened the book, reading the words covering the page which he had once wanted her to see. They hit him with a force he could barely stand as he read each word, seeing her in his mind. Finished reading, he closed the book, his chest constricting until he could barely breathe.

A few hours later, Harrold came in, his arm now in a sling to isolate his shoulder. He had demanded to be released from the doctor's care when he had heard that Burke was packing. For the first time, he thought bitterly, his station had finally seemed to mean something. He looked at Burke, watching him as he placed his belongings in his pack, remaining silent despite feeling Harrold's eyes on him. Harrold reached down, touching the books on her nightstand, then seeing something else Burke had not taken. He nodded as Burke noticed Maeve's rosary, resting on the cloth beside her lamp.

Harrold bowed his head, frowning. "Burke…"

"I'm taking her body back to London. The RAMC notified her mother. She is arranging the service. I should be in England by then."

Burke paused, looking at him, his eyes piercing, a visible fury burning just beneath the surface. He nodded at the rosary. "She'd want you to have it," he said evenly. Harrold stared at him, a strange expression appearing across his face as he watched Burke quietly, seeing a brutality in him he only once might have believed existed. Now it loomed with full force, as though coursing through him like poisoned and acidic blood.

"Burke…"

Burke shook his head. "All these years since the war started, I never believed in God." He then chortled bitterly to himself. "And now if He does exist, I'll be cursing Him all the way from hell."

Harrold tried to speak, but no words came. Burke saw the Englishman's expression. He then picked up his bags and walked toward the door, pausing next to Harrold, knowing neither of them knew what to say. Both stood in silence for several moments, then, raising his head to look outside, while Harrold bowed his head, Burke left, heading for the transport.

∞

Burke stood quietly on the deck of the ship leaving Le Havre to cross the short distance of the channel to Southampton. Loads of baggage from the group of passengers had finished loading only minutes before, the last among them Maeve's coffin, covered in ropes as the stewards hauled it into the chasm below the boat decks.

The wind moaned as it flowed against the cold, churning gray water of the sea. He closed his eyes, hearing the low, deep tones of Maeve's voice, still so clear in his mind. He had heard it, too, in the camp as he had stared at the simple coffin covered by both a British and an American flag, surrounded by medical officers and soldiers, staring upon it and remembering the woman who lay inside. The camp's Anglican chaplain recited a passage from the *Book of Common Prayer* as a priest also stood nearby, the nurses and doctors pausing in the frenzy of activity and carnage to pay their respects. Few of them had known her outside of her presence in the camp, the smoothness of her voice having been heard by the countless souls who had passed through the canvas walls of the surgery.

Harrold had remained several feet away from Burke as the chaplain gave his final benediction, sending his temporary flock on their way as several soldiers carried her body to an awaiting Red Cross vehicle. He had said nothing, seeing Burke in another world, consumed by a deep-seated and unexpressed agony. No one else said anything to him but a few words of simple condolence, knowing that he wouldn't have tolerated anything else lest level one of her mourners with a few carefully chosen words. The only thing Harrold could do was stay back, as he had before, reminding Burke of his presence. Even then, his show of silent commiseration remained unnoticed, as Burke had isolated himself even more in the last hours. Harrold had watched him silently, his own emotions having been erratic, his memory a minefield unto itself, shattering him with moments that played themselves endlessly until his own façade cracked, leaving him helpless to combat them. There was no one but Burke who would have understood, but even so, Harrold knew he was unreachable and was sinking irretrievably into the depths of his own mind.

Within the last days, the Allied camp had been informed of countless German retreats, an Armistice undoubtedly to follow. In the interim, Harrold knew he would soon be home, faced with his wife and children, including a new child who would be born within weeks of his arrival. The thought of it sickened him, the thought of his own seed living and breathing when he himself now only identified with death. He now understood why men could never return to their former lives without being haunted by the men they had become. Nothing would ever be the same. And where it concerned her life, he could only believe her death had been his responsibility.

Burke stood on a London street, watching several people entering an Anglican church in Kensington, their umbrellas up to guard against a steady rain which began to fall. An older woman stood, presiding over the gathering of mourners. She was coldly aristocratic, unapproachable, her features perfect and aquiline like those of an American Brahmin, holding out her hand in a cloying gesture of thanks as those among her British friends came to offer her a few kind words over the death of her only daughter. She resembled Maeve only slightly, just enough so that he knew that the only thing that bound them together was blood. In every other way she seemed to be the antithesis of who her daughter had been, a shell of a human being compared to the strong woman whose quietness masked a deep fire within. It was a slow, strange fire which even now continued to exist, the memory of it continuing to burn through him like a poison, a poison which had been born of regret and the pain that came from his belief that he had failed to love her enough to keep her safe.

Burke watched as the last of the mourners went inside, followed by Evelyn O'Hanlon and the Anglican priest who was presiding over the service. Burke bowed his head, continuing to be soaked by the storm. He made no attempt to walk across the chasm between where he stood and the church where Maeve now would be held captive by those people, many of whom she hadn't known in addition to those whom she had so long ago managed to leave behind.

He waited until a few hours later, after everyone had gone. He entered the church. Candles were still lit from the memorial service, now half spent, the chapel empty except for the casket, resting at the end of the long stretch of red carpet extending between the pews. Burke walked slowly toward it, his eyes glistening. The casket would be left for only a few more hours, burial taking place only when it could, as the cemeteries were growing more full with the extent of the country's dead, each having to wait sometimes days before it would find its place in the ground. Had she had her wish, she would have been cremated like her father, and taken back to the same place from which it seems both of their families had originally come. It was only after her death that he found that her father's family, before moving to Armagh, had also come from within several miles of where he had been born, and where his ashes had been scattered on the dark, high rock of the Cliffs of Moher.

Burke approached her quietly. Even though he had looked upon her only days before, seeing her now jarred him, the sight of her body laid out inside, her eyes closed, dressed in the kind of clothing he had never seen her wear. It was apparent that someone who didn't know her had attempted to place her among the cold, aristocratic notions of upper-class propriety her mother had tried to create for her even in these last moments. Had she known, he knew she would have seen it as an abomination.

He turned, looking around him, taking in the church's decoration, the pulpit, the rich ornamentation which seemed to cover every inch of the walls and ceilings, ornate velvet and silk, symbols in brocade which shone against a solid background of crimson. A large cross hung in the center focal point, raised high and covered in gold. To him they could only be the harsh and superficial displays of a world bearing no resemblance to the reality he had known. Instead it seemed a cruel realm of seductive and numbing fantasy geared toward those who would forever walk if even a step away from the meaning of a living, visceral hell.

He turned back to her, looking at her clothing and her body at rest. Nothing of him would remain with her the moment her body entered the ground. The thought caused a wave of nausea to move over him as the blood drained from his face. He felt himself become shaky, his body shivering. He reached into his pocket, pulling from it something he had meant to give her when he had returned from the line, and when the war was over. It was a single antique band which had belonged to his own grandmother, intricate designs carved into it. He steadied himself, breathing deeply as he slowly placed it on her finger, watching as it slipped easily into place. He then reached down, kissing her gently on the lips. He lingered, feeling the taut coldness of her skin. He then pulled away, his eyes glistening. "I sent for this from Lahinch when I first saw you. Until now I didn't have the courage."

He bowed his head, looking at her, touching her face. Water from the rain on his coat fell onto her body. In the light of the church, falling drops from his hair also masked the tears on his face, which for the first time he allowed to fall. But, he thought, after leaving, he would not allow himself to do so again. Such a time had come and gone, as though even the last parts of himself which he recognized as human were being buried with her.

He then turned, his body dead, numb, his expression hard and full of hatred as he stared long into the heart of the church, as though he were staring into the face of God. He paused, his deep voice trembling with anger and a pain which continued its merciless deadening of whatever warmth remained.

"Damn you for taking her, you sonofabitch—" he whispered bitterly. "She was the only reason to stay alive."

Harrold sat forward in a chair by the fire as he stared out into space. His body was thin, worn, suddenly out of place where he would have before fit in perfectly. His wife and her father in a vapid discussion, cold commentary which was the equivalent of gossip among their group of acquaintances as they solidified plans for the coming weeks with Harrold finally home, his having been granted medical leave after Burke had left the front. Harrold had barely noticed, not able to have concentrated on much since his arrival, his mind having been trained solely on the events of the last few weeks. He knew Burke was still in town, having received a telegraphed message before Harrold had arrived in England from the port in Le Havre.

Harrold returned to the present moment and tuned in to their conversation. After only a few words, he knew he wouldn't be able to stand it, and he rose, walking to the hallway where he collected his hat and overcoat, bent on escaping before anyone realized he was gone.

As he was about to open the door, his wife entered the foyer. She was a handsome woman, the living, if cold, replica of the photograph Harrold had carried with him at the front. Even now, standing before him she was perfectly attired and carried herself in such a way as to remind him, less than subtly, of their position in society. She stood before him, her gaze fixed on his hand, still poised on the door handle. She frowned, her voice cold.

"Harrold, just where do you think you're going?" She stared at him, expecting an answer.

He turned to her briefly as he opened the door. "I'm going out."

Harrold looked at her a moment longer in irritation and closed the door behind him as he walked out onto the street, leaving her and her father behind.

    Burke and Harrold sat at a small table in the bar of the Connaught Hotel. Both were silent, as Burke ordered another whisky, hardly touching it when it was placed before him, the barkeep looking at the two strangely, not knowing where they both had just come from, as though to see either of them at the same table should have been absurd.

    Harrold looked at him closely. "So what are you going to do now?"

    "I don't know. I thought I'd go back to Paris."

    Harrold felt a slow anger rising in his chest. His voice was low as he leveled himself at the man before him, the sound of his own demons ringing with an unfamiliar strength in his ears.

    "Damn you, Burke...you weren't the only one who loved her." The raw pain suddenly pushed beneath the sudden severity with which he had just berated the man who had somehow become his friend, and he calmed himself, staring at the brandy he had ordered without any desire to drink it. He pushed it to the side. "What good is it going to do to have you rotting away in Paris? She wouldn't have wanted that."

    Burke turned away, his voice rough, slurred from the shots of whiskey he had done before the Englishman's arrival. "I should have been on the base. I shouldn't have gone to the line." He bowed his head, as Harrold watched him silently. "Her own countrymen killed them—even someone else took care of that."

    Harrold turned to Burke, his eyes piercing. "As though you could have done anything, you selfish bastard." He then paused, his voice dropping angrily. "At least you were spared one thing, Burke, you didn't have to watch her die." They sat in silence for a few moments, Harrold's eyes glistening. "What the hell will you do in Paris?"

"I don't know."

Harrold frowned. "You'll tire of it one day—expatriates and goddamned pacifists who never saw the front but nevertheless claim to be experts on it drinking themselves incoherent and bedding every whore they can get their hands on." He then paused, staring at the Irishman. "So what will you do when you have enough?"

"I don't know," he said disagreeably. "Disappear."

Harrold smiled bitterly. "I won't hear from you. Nor will I ever know that you produced another earnest word. They might have been the only thing which would save you." He put his glass down on the table, staring at Burke as though seeing through him. "None of us has come back without our demons, my friend, and the worst part of it is no one gives a damn."

Burke looked him in the eye for the first time, his eyes cold, lifeless. Harrold started at the darkness there.

Burke then bowed his head and turned, walking out the door of the hotel, leaving Harrold sitting alone in the bar, watching him as he walked away.

Harrold had been back home for several hours, sitting silently in his leather chair in the library. He stared into the flames of the fire one of the servants had lit, having anticipated he would retreat to the one place he could find solitude as he had every evening since his arrival back in London. There he had managed to escape from everyone and everything that would have unceremoniously attempted to bring him back to a world they thought he should have embraced with open arms. Thoughts of the years since he had been home haunted him, and not for having missed it. Instead it was an unexplainable torment to be met with the familiar and be expected to embrace it. From Nairobi to the front near Amiens, he had dreaded this moment of returning to the expectations of the men and women who knew nothing of him but that to which he was supposed to give the most allegiance. Hearth and home, society, and damp, cold mornings spent walking the familiar path taken by his progenitors since the family had existed. Places where he would be welcomed not for who he was, but for whom he was supposed to have been, with the same constancy and lack of any emotion which accompanied men of his station. And among them was the woman who, for better or for worse, was his wife, whom he knew would soon be coming to stand behind him, the typical look of disapproval and disappointment leveled against him, and without an ounce of compassion one would hope to expect from even basic civility one would offer a complete stranger. He laughed to himself, seeing the expression he anticipated in his mind. A moment later, he turned, seeing whom he had supposed was indeed where he had expected she would be.

"Where have you been?" Her tone was mercenary, as much as was her expression. She walked into the study, facing him. "You were gone for several hours, Harrold. I had thought—quite stupid of me—that once you got back we would return to some sense of normalcy. If not for your own sake, then certainly for mine."

Harrold frowned, turning back to the fire.

Gladys frowned, her tone clipped. "You have responsibilities, Harrold. If not to me, then at least to your family, and then your station. How does it look to have you here night after night, refusing to be seen—holing yourself up here in this room? One would think you actually preferred the battlefield to being home here among your friends and family. It would stand to reason that such behavior is contrary to all that these men just coming home have fought for."

Harrold laughed at the rabid ignorance of her comment, responding by taking another pronounced swig of Scotch. Gladys stared at him. "Harrold, answer me—without sitting there as though you were made of stone."

He turned to her, his tone even. "I'm not the man you married, Gladys. All of those years... Nor will I ever be again." He then shook his head to himself, responding to the absurdity that accompanied his own tone, the truth of what he was about to say already ringing in his ears. "No matter what parties we attend, what functions at which you think we need to be seen, what new blood you wish to add to our ever-dwindling station in society, you will be married to a man who, from this moment on, ceases to give a damn."

Gladys paused for several moments, her expression turning hawkish. "Then I shall assume I will be going to our friends' houses and dinner parties alone. Including the one planned for this evening, welcoming you home." She turned to leave the room, and then, thinking better of it, looked at him again, her usual coldness further pronounced. "And should anyone ask, I shall tell them that my husband died during the war. It seems you have already."

Harrold remained silent, listening as Gladys left. He took another drink and continued staring into the fire.

He could hear her calling to him, the soft strength of her voice carried on the winds which for the last several days had battered the steep black cliffs near Lahinch, black rock dropping sharply to the sea below. He could see nothing but the mist over the water, the ocean churning, its waves crashing against the shore. The sound became like thunder in his ears, louder and louder until he could barely breathe, the sound reverberating sharply through his body, until he could hear nothing else.

Moments later he was walking through a bombed-out field, seeing before him a wasteland of bodies and charred earth underneath his feet. All around him was the mist of early dawn, the light not yet fully over the horizon, coalescing with gas which hung heavily in the air, casting a gray-blue sheen over everything in sight. Misshapen bodies rested in the deep-pitted black earth, rotted, torn flesh filled with maggots, halves of skulls blown away, hands in claw-

*like forms reaching forward, frozen, men's eyes wide open
in horror, their skin taut and drawn like death masks.*
*He then heard her voice again, haunted by its strange, deep
softness as a figure moved toward him, her hair down over
her shoulders, her body in silhouette. She was leading a
horse, gleaming white in the fog, a rare, perfect shaft of
light streaming behind her.*
       "Maeve…"

       Burke awakened suddenly, rising in the bed. He
tried to catch his breath, awakening enough to feel his body
shuddering, his skin covered with sweat. He closed his eyes,
feeling the first rays of daylight as they shone through the
window. The sky outside was gray and overcast, even at
dawn. Rain had fallen for the last several days, and would
continue, pools of brackish water having covered the streets,
men and women bustling from place to place without
looking at anyone or anything, as though trying to escape.
Burke had instead walked without even feeling the hard
sheets of rain, almost missing the mud of the trenches, the
company of other men, the terse jokes and commentary
before dawn. He had only left his hotel a few times to walk
the streets, and even then he was not sure where he was
going. Men and women had stared at him as though he
were a ghost, looking into his rough, masculine face and the
hollowness in his gray-green eyes.
       He was scheduled to leave the next morning for
Paris, crossing the same channel that had brought Maeve's
body to her mother in London. In his own mind, it would
be the same as returning home.
       A few hours later, once again he walked quietly on
the sidewalk, his head down, his breath visible in the dank
morning air. He stared ahead, unblinking, hearing the faint
sound of music in the distance. His breath was shallow as he
recognized it. He turned and found a church conducting
services, the sound of the choir singing the opening lines of

"Jerusalem," commemorating the landscape and the glory of England. In his ears the music was low, hollow, and in his mind full of hypocrisy, as though taunting him from the impenetrable fortress of gray stone. Anger steeped irrevocably within him until every fiber was infused with hatred. No other emotion, he knew, would offer him solace.

Had she been with him, she would have been able to reach within him, eradicating whatever emotion now sought to destroy him. She had been the other part of his soul, the one voice outside of his own who could have saved him from the hell that had moved through him since her death. Again, he could feel even more now than before as though he had already died, his body the only thing which continued to hold him, now dragging him into a melancholy from which he did not want to awaken. But she was gone, gone to the God in whom her father had taught her to believe.

∞

Burke sat at the long, polished oak table in a boardroom, facing a stern, middle-aged bishop who referred silently to a small stack of documents. The room was cold, rain falling outside as it had for the last days. Around him were the trappings of Catholicism, rich furnishings, polished oak and hardwood.

"You understand that once you sign these papers, the property you have will no longer exist. Your holdings, anything of any value, we will take as an offering to the Church, and in return you will be given sanctuary in a small hermitage on the grounds of the Prieuré de Sainte Marie near Foix. At no time shall you be turned from the property. However, should you leave of your own accord you will not be able to claim anything from us to make your way elsewhere. Your offering is irrevocable."

Burke looked at him quietly, hearing the solemnity

of his tone. He frowned, nodding. "I understand."

The bishop then nodded. He offered him a pen, watching as Burke signed the document put before him in silence. The bishop peered at him, as though trying to discern why he would choose the course he had, as it was evident the Irishman was lacking in everything he would normally have expected in a man seeking to devote his life to contemplation. Instead he saw a man existing in past memory and bitterness, a coldness which seemed to have rendered him purposefully invulnerable so as not to feel anything in the presence of anyone else, much less the men before him. Anyone who might have seen him in that moment could easily feel the inward brutality and rage which existed just beneath the surface.

The bishop watched as Burke finished signing the documents, then handed the bishop his pen, remaining silent. The bishop breathed deeply, accepting them, and handing them to a priest who stood just behind him. "You must understand that an arrangement such as this does not relieve you of the contemplation that would be necessary to be granted true absolution for your sins," he said quietly, staring into the Irishman's face, as though out of habit searching for some kind of penitence. "If I may ask—why would a man choose to live the rest of his life in the Church when his experiences have left him with so little faith?"

Burke smiled caustically, his voice even, not attempting to hide his contempt. "I am at war, Father," he said. "And I always will be."

PART TWO
THE ARIEGE, FRANCE 1919

The Field is red with poppy flowers
Where mushroom meadows stand
It's only seven fairy hours
From there to Fairyland
Now when the star shells riot up
In flares of red and green,
Each Fairy leaves her buttercup
And goes to see her Queen.

Where little ghostly moonbeams glow
Through mushroom alleys white
The Fairies carry on their way
A glow-worm lamp for Light.
Now when I see the glow worm light
In boyau seventeen
I know the Fairy goes that night
To see the Fairy Queen.

-- Anonymous (1916)

    Burke observed his new surroundings as the taxi traveled slowly along the road. Outside he saw the countryside of southwestern Gascony with its rocky hills and dark forests, the sky darkened from a front moving in from the northwest. Already he knew that he was in a different land, as even the air was different, a strange charge in the wind, the Pyrenees looming in the distance.

    Ahead was the façade of the monastery, standing tall against the expanse of overcast sky, its bleached gray limestone weathered and worn, cracked and covered with ivy. Its windows were small, dark, while outside the figures of darkly cowled monks walked from the monastery around the grounds or worked steadily in silence.

He had hired the horse-drawn transport in the village, handing his last few francs and centimes marked with the visible insignia of the Republique Française. The old man who had agreed to take him had refused at first, but Burke had silently placed the money in his hands for going several miles out of his way. The old man had looked at him silently and with few words accepted, helping the Celt into the small wagon and driving through the hills along the narrow unpaved road, after perhaps two hours finally reaching the forest that marked the beginning of the priory grounds. Burke had withstood the journey, refusing to think or to allow any emotion to reach through his rough-hewn façade.

His meeting with the bishop had happened a few days before, after which he had made his way toward one of the several bars he had frequented during the war. The streets were filled with soldiers, men who would soon be on their way back home to the villages and towns both in France and abroad. There was a strangeness in the air he had noticed the moment he had arrived on the train, an almost insidious undercurrent to victory, as though the city were rapt with a mixture of relief and displacement. The displacement had manifested as a rootlessness, a restlessness which had come from no one knowing what should or would happen next. He had seen the look in the soldiers' eyes, hollow and without emotion. Civilians were celebrating more out of relief than victory as former soldiers, poilu, discharged from duty, stood watching. Many of them were disabled, several of them without limbs, standing on the side of the road or seated in makeshift wheelchairs. A few were even without faces, their visages mangled, an eye or jaw missing. Despite hiding themselves, he could see them turn away in horror and shame as they elicited terrified looks from small children. Burke saw the sadness in their eyes, former soldiers whose own bodies had betrayed them, and worse, would forever remind them of the hell which now left them with only the memory of who they once had been.

Burke wandered inside the bar, the first thing in his line of sight being several prostitutes drunk and leaning against the wall, listening with amusement to some old Frenchman singing the Marseillaise. Men sat beside them, pouring drinks and muttering to one another, nodding to the crowds outside. Burke found a place away from all of them, watching as a bartender moved over to him, carrying a bottle of whisky. The bartender placed it before him, nodding to the wall. Burke saw several pages of yellowed articles, a few which carried his byline. He opened the bottle and poured the Scotch into a glass, watching as the bartender went back toward the bar. He then swigged the whisky, staring at the faces of the men and women as they drank, watching with amusement as others outside continued to celebrate. It was then that he realized that even though the world would go on, for some the war would never end.

The Irishman stepped slowly from the wagon, seeing a young monk who had come outside to greet him. The boy was perhaps seventeen, dark eyes and hair, dressed in a dark brown robe with a high collar to protect him from the morning's dampness. Speaking with a heavy Basque-accented French, the boy bowed slightly.

"The Abbot is waiting for you, Monsieur." His young voice was light, innocent, as he smiled at the Irishman. "I'll show you to him."

The boy nodded to the driver, who got back inside the wagon, and seeing the statue of the Virgin which marked the priory entrance, crossed himself as he drove away. The young monk then turned back to Burke, motioning toward the door. The Irishman picked up his bag and followed him inside.

Burke walked quietly behind the boy taking in their surroundings as they made their way to the abbot's office. Around him were the east and south ranges, inside which were the scriptoria, the calefactory and the ambulatory—the long, vaulted processional hallway into which various rooms and other hallways opened. There was also a starkness which was oddly appealing, almost beautiful, though he could feel the strangeness of the atmosphere, with the walls standing amidst an artificially imposed silence. Each monk who passed was busy in his duties, though many of them nodded a greeting. Each of them moved with an air of regimentation, as though any observed idleness would be met with condemnation. Such, he thought, bitterly, and with a caustic amusement, were the armies of God.

"I take it you've been treated well upon your arrival."

Burke nodded, as the abbot turned behind him, smiling slightly as he poured them both a rich, local Armagnac, its amber color catching the light. Lascaux moved smoothly, handing him a crystal snifter. Burke remained silent, accepting the specialized brandy as the older Frenchman turned, facing him more fully. The abbot was in his mid-sixties, a tall man with olive skin and piercing gray eyes. He was more refined than Burke would have expected, as though he were from some ancient family who had preferred isolation from the rest of the world, untouched by modern sensibilities out of conscious choice rather than from ignorance of their existence, as though preferring to remain irretrievably locked in the past.

Lascaux watched as Burke continued staring absently into the room, out of habit taking in his surroundings. The Irishman was haggard, unshaven, his clothes looking as though he had come from a brothel, little better than the uniform Lascaux knew he had worn several weeks before. The abbot smiled to himself. "You will be ready soon, I assume, to go into the seclusion from whence you will be cleansed of whatever sins were committed before you came here. It is what will be expected of you."

Burke nodded again. "The bishop told you why I was coming."

"Only as much as he believed relevant. It isn't often that we receive someone from Ireland—though I know you have spent much of your time in France. In terms of your home country, perhaps one or two priests in the last twenty years who have come on retreat. It should be an interesting experience for us all." Lascaux stood next to the window, looking outside at several of the monks attending to their gardens. "I suggest that while you are here, you live your life studiously in the pursuit of Truth. Contemplation is something which we encourage quite strongly, as there is not one of us who cannot benefit from knowing ourselves, and our God, better." He turned, seeing Burke looking at him quietly. "Often many of our friars find that Nature is a tremendous boon to that cause—as in the breast of Nature a man finds the wonders of the Divine in their most affecting state."

Burke remained silent, watching the abbot pause, his manner now less contemplative as he turned back toward the Celt.

"You will be placed in a hermitage two days from now," Lascaux continued. "Normally one would be forced to wait two or three years before they would be ready for seclusion, but the archdiocese in Paris asked that we make an exception in your case. Perhaps they thought solitude would be a healing influence for one of your experiences, and an appropriate place to seek absolution. As you know, absolution is more than the forgiveness of sin through confession. It is also an accompanying eradication of guilt and fear. When one finds the Divine, he will no longer know either of these emotions, and will instead find the peace that comes from Divine grace. That is what you must seek."

Burke bowed his head, again listening to the abbot's comments as though they had been recited a thousand times until becoming rote, the only difference being his attention to speaking distinctly for the benefit of belaboring an upcoming point.

Lascaux continued, looking at him quietly. "The war wreaked havoc on your conscience as it has with many who came before you and had similar experiences. Such men need a place to mend their souls. You have been sent here to meet yourself through God and know truly what He intends. It is my hope you will find just such solace here—and know His will in such isolation."

Burke entered the small cell inside the tower where he had been placed until he could be taken to the hermitage the following day. It also housed the quarters of Lascaux and some of the older friars, each of whom occupied a single room away from the rest of the younger men and novitiates.

The floor, walls and ceiling were made of the same stone. A single, small window overlooked the grounds. The furnishings were spare, the starkness of the room appropriate for its purposeful lack of distraction. His mattress lay on the ground, beside it a single table on which sat a basin of water, a pitcher and a bar of rough, homemade soap made out of lard. Burke walked over to the mattress, easing himself onto it after several days without sleep, relaxing for the first time since his arrival. Without thought or emotion he lay silently, listening to the wind against the stone.

A monk approached Burke's room just before dawn, knocking quietly. He waited for Burke to collect his few belongings and come outside. They made their way silently down the path from the priory, entering a section of the grounds which Burke had seen from his window. Around them stood the ancient forest of oak, ash, and blackthorn, growing in their own, sheltered twilight, rays of normally sparse sunlight beaming through the leaves, illuminating in brilliant shards the darkness of the wood.

There were few other souls there that morning, the monks who wandered before matins looked at them briefly with vague interest before turning back to the path and to the silence of their prayers.

It was an hour later that Burke and the monk reached the hermitage. It was a small, one room stone structure, nestled on the edge of the forest. The old monk paused, turning to him curtly, speaking for the first time since retrieving him from his cell.

"I am to leave you now to get settled. Provisions will be brought once a week to the small shed at the edge of the grounds. Yours and the other retreatant's will be clearly marked. Should you need anything in particular, indicate it on the log which is to be left inside. The brothers will see to your request if it is feasible."

Burke frowned. "The other retreatant?"

A strange irritation seeming to move through the monk as he nodded toward the forest. "There is another man who shares these woods. Monsieur de Gascogne. Do not seek him out. He is also in seclusion following his service in the war."

The monk opened the door, standing aside, as though to allow Burke room to enter. Burke paused, then moved forward, standing just inside the doorway. He then looked back, seeing the monk standing silently, nodding a curt acknowledgment.

Burke turned to the entrance of the hermitage. Like his cell in the abbey, the room was spare, boasting nothing but dirt floor, a small bed and wool blanket. A perfunctory table rested against one wall, facing a fireplace in which was poised a small iron pot for cooking and a kettle which sat on the hearth.

Burke closed his eyes, feeling a ray of sunlight on his face which shone through the window. In his silent reverie he lost time. There was no past and no future, nothing but the sound of an ancient wind, striking as it had in the abbey, against wood and stone.

The monk opened the large wooden door, having heard the knocker from all the way down the hall in one of the several sitting rooms. Gascogne stood, watching the elderly monk's body bow silently in reverence as he let him in the door.

Lascaux was working at his desk, looking through various correspondence when his young assistant knocked at the door, entering and waiting patiently as Lascaux finished what he was doing. Lascaux looked up, seeing a young monk looking at him expectantly.

"What is it...?"

The boy bowed his head, not looking into the abbot's eyes. "Chrétien de Gascogne, Father. He's waiting for you outside."

Lascaux breathed deeply, leaning back in his chair. He stared at the boy, frowning, then motioning for him to open the door. "Show him in."

The boy opened the door, standing aside. Gascogne stood silently, staring at Lascaux without ceremony. The young monk watched the tall, once handsome Frenchman, his manner even and silent, as though waiting for the abbot to make his purpose known for having disturbed his seclusion.

The abbot spoke, addressing Gascogne quietly. "Sit, make yourself comfortable."

Gascogne sat, remaining silent. Lascaux then addressed the boy, who stood watching the two men nervously.

"You may go."

The young man paused, watching the two older men staring at one another, as though locked in a silent duel. He then bowed his head, and with a short nod, ducked outside the door, closing it dutifully behind him.

Lascaux paused, sizing up the Frenchman before him. Gascogne had grown thinner over the last months, his skin paler, whether it was from the change of season or something else, Lascaux didn't know, but out of respect for the aristocrat's position, felt it would have been inappropriate to ask. As a man home from war, he had known any number of maladies would have been possible.

"It has been a long time, Monsieur de Gascogne."

Gascogne simply nodded.

"There is a man who has just arrived here from the front. We've taken him in for retreat, and he has entered seclusion near your hermitage. He was sent here by the archdiocese in Paris."

"What does that have to do with me?"

"He is an Irishman, and despite being Catholic, from what the bishop has suggested, he does not seem to willingly embrace the Church. Why they would send him here, I don't know, except that it seemed they thought he would welcome a place such as this to seek absolution. He gave all of his possessions, whatever could be construed as such, to the Church in return for that privilege."

Lascaux stood, offering Gascogne some brandy, which Gascogne refused.

"From what I understand, he was one of the more respected journalists covering the western front. My fear is that this is a man who has faced experiences no man should ever have seen, and it has caused him to feel a great deal of contempt—perhaps enough to castigate God on his own ground. He certainly has the intelligence so that he would be among those who consider faith to be an exercise in semantics."

Gascogne frowned, remaining silent.

"I thought it best to warn you. It is possible that he would seek to compare experiences according to his own misbegotten sense of morality. My hope is that he will not attempt to find solace in your company, but instead use this as an opportunity to seek the will of God." Lascaux paused, his irritation at the presence of one who would show such a lack of devotion subtly apparent. "My suggestion would be that you stay away from him if you should happen to come across him on the grounds."

Gascogne looked at him pointedly, his expression cold. "I won't go to his part of the grounds. But I'll make no promises should he happen to find his way to mine."

∞

Burke entered his hermitage, taking off the long, rough cloak and placing it on the table beside the door. He had been for a walk among the grounds, unable to withstand the penetrating silence of the small stone structure he would now consider home. Every moment in even the first day had been an eternity. He chortled to himself, thinking that should he take the time to imbibe all of the Armagnac in France, it would only last him a few weeks. He immediately reached for a bottle of wine, one of several which had been left for him in the hermitage, which he had saved for his return. He opened the bottle, taking a swig. He walked over to the chair before the fire, sitting as he stoked the remaining embers. Within moments the thick red wine hit his stomach, rising in him like a heat. He could feel the familiar warmth wash over him as he closed his eyes, allowing the drunkenness to soothe him like a balm, erasing the thoughts from his mind. For a moment the pain began to deaden, and he longed to slip further into the blackness of some mindless reverie, laughing to himself about the absurdity of the fact that he was still alive.

He opened his eyes and glanced at the mantle above the fireplace. Two objects remained from the front, both of them having to do with her. One was the photograph of her standing before a British Red Cross vehicle, staring wryly into the camera. The sight of her immediately produced pain. He could feel her, the softness of her skin and the warmth of her body as she had lain beside him. But more painful still was the memory of her voice, reverberating through his mind with its soft, warm depth, reaching effortlessly that place no one else had ever been able to reach. It had amazed him that someone so inherently a woman didn't think of herself in those terms, and instead thought of herself as the soul who loved him. Perhaps that was why she had commanded the surgical unit so easily, and why no one had ever seemed to intimidate her, the very simple lack of fear of their disapproval allowed her to continue moving forward in her own direction, whether or not they gave a damn. But even this was, to a certain extent, whom she had shown the world. Only he had seen inside of her, having touched the one part of her soul no one else had ever seen or perhaps knew existed. It was the same sensation he had felt the moment he stared into her eyes, and he was suddenly reminded of who he was. The only thing he knew was that he had been destined to find her, and that, God be damned, he would not rest until he was with her again.

Next to her photo lay her copy of *An Choiméide Dhiaga*. The irony of it and its presence moved through him with an absurdity which he knew even now would haunt him, as though it would have been intended by her had she known, had some part of her, even in death, as one of the two personal belongings of any importance she had kept. Such thoughts drove men mad, he thought bitterly, that no one on earth, in heaven or amidst the infernos of hell could find some reason behind the madness of moments which had the power to drive a man toward his own destruction. He had taken everything which had been cast upon him in life, from the horror of war itself to the subsequent depths of man's depravity, and still—it was her memory which haunted him, knowing he would never recover, and nor did he have any desire to be relieved from such ensuing moments of pain. She had long ago made room in her soul so that he could reside there with her, as her father had when she was a child. And he would not give up that space in his soul in which she would exist, along with the pain that made him remember. Within moments, he had taken another swig of wine, closing his eyes, letting himself sit until the warmth had enough of a weightlessness to wash any thoughts of her aside, except those for which he could easily control. He then began to laugh drunkenly, thinking with sudden irony that with so much time to think, the idea of death itself, as he sat now in his isolated hell, would become so bitterly and coarsely poetic.

Gascogne rested on his knees against the coldness of the dirt floor. The room was dark, with only a single candle lit in the corner of the room. His body shook, having remained unmoving for over an hour, his body already weakened from the war having become wracked with pain, his muscles cramped and throbbing from having kneeled for so long without comfort on the ground.

He stared absently out the window, feeling his body failing him. The sky had become a slate gray, light piercing the high atmosphere as the thunderheads moved east. He could smell the charge in the wind, knowing what it meant, as a breeze started to strike against the hermitage. He smiled, knowing that within moments the rain would begin to fall, the faint, but ominous sound of thunder in the distance. In the window pane, he could see his reflection, the long, almost gaunt body which had once been so strong, and the scars which covered his face. Months earlier, had he seen this image, he would not have recognized himself. But the months since the war had taken their toll, rendering him to the state of existence which no man would choose to withstand should he indeed have had any choice. His body was slowly deteriorating, breaking down in exhaustive increments which he could feel as the days passed, and sometimes even from moment to moment, as though life itself were reminding him that he was indeed mortal. The vestments he continued to wear had covered his body enough that Lascaux had not been able to see the full extent of his condition, and it was what he would have wanted. In remembering the years which had passed, and what had happened during those years, the effects had been inevitable. But it was not something he had expected the abbot to understand. Even for a man of God, he could not have known what it was like watching the moments which seemed like an eternity between life and death, as though the world itself had slowed almost to a stop the moment someone was killed before a man's eyes in the brutal reality of the temporal world. In that same moment, a man could only wonder if he would take the next bullet or fragment of shrapnel, and if such would be enough to kill him just as brutally. He remembered well the priests who had gone into battle with the men themselves, and these were the men who then understood all too well why men either chose to cling to God and faith or otherwise had chosen to despise Him. For they themselves, he knew, could only have had their own dark nights of the soul, however it might have seemed otherwise, watching brave men die. Any man who hadn't, no matter what he might have shown to the outside world, could not have been human.

Gascogne paused, feeling the blood coursing through his body, the coldness of the air feeling strangely good against his skin, for it reminded him that he indeed still lived, and would perhaps live long enough to see another day. Too many nights had passed when he had felt the congestion in his lungs, both lobes damaged by gas which had fallen over successive weeks on the line, having known since leaving the front that his body itself would slowly begin to fail. Each moment, despite his pain, seemed a strange blessing, not knowing how long, whether it would be weeks or months, before he slowly succumbed. When the night came, he would remember the days that had brought him to this point, believing that even such moments had been for a reason. And it was more than whatever faith he had had as a child. It was something else. Looking out the window, he could see the night descending. In that last light, he could feel every moment of his past, as though God himself had wanted him to trace every moment, every part of his path until it all had become clear. Perhaps then, in the most important ways imaginable, and in whatever resonance which came so poignantly with remembrance, he would have truly found a way to heal.

He remembered the fields, the trenches filled with French troops from the Fourth Army who were stationed in Champagne near the Marne, facing down Below's First Army. Gouraud had anticipated the German movement, and had planned for it, though it meant sacrificing the first line of soldiers, knowing that they would be the immediate target as the French troops went on the offensive. The Germans in 1916 had won enough ground that they had no compunction in terms of leveling everything they could upon the line, and Gouraud had determined the best means to strike first, even with fewer batteries of artillery than those which were facing the French battalions. Using what became known as the *ligne de sacrifice* to gain the advantage, it was a courageous, but otherwise necessarily brutal move, if only to shake German confidence in a surprise maneuver as the Germans attempted to gain further ground. For the men themselves were to be sacrificed for the offensive, he knew few would make it out alive.

Gascogne had stood watching the carnage before him, the earth itself seeming to swallow the fallen as the offensive commenced in the night air. Soldiers called to one another in every conceivable language and dialect amidst the thick waves of chalk dust, smoke and gas, screaming across the roars of machine guns and field artillery, their faces covered with sweat and blood. The firestorm continued across the field, men killed instantly as the mortars exploded through the trenches, sending sand and earth in all directions, several of the men with barely enough time to scream as they were instantly blown apart in a spray of blood.

Gascogne had been in the forward area, unable to

stay in the rear, despite orders, feeling the need to be with his own soldiers, and in particular the ones who were to be sacrificed, until as many of his men as possible could fall back. He had moved through the communications trench to the front lines, a rifle in his hands as he watched the section of line to the north. He could hear the blast of long-range guns, and the sound of mortars slicing through the air, ending in a low moan as it suddenly ripped through the ground and exploded on impact before them. Several men fell within the radius of several hundred feet, and instantly he felt the hot shards of metal ripping through the flesh on his own body. Beside him was another of his troops, his eyes open and fixed, half of his body torn away, while smoke moved in a slow wave across the field, an eerie glow in the night against the fires which had started from the blast. Time had suddenly slowed down, and his mind had fallen into a haze as thick as the smoke around him. The pain was unbearable, flesh ripped and nerves exposed to the gas-filled air. Deafened by the blast, the only thing he could hear was the thunder of blood in his veins and the distant sounds of the battle raging in the background, the cold air against his skin, as amidst the darkness, the dead continued to fall.

Gascogne felt himself begin to lose consciousness. It was the slow, engulfing haze that made him realize that he no longer felt pain, instead feeling only a strange warmth move through him, as though he were being lulled into a state from which he knew he might not awaken. He then came to realize he was dying, as his eyes began to close, the warmth making him want desperately to give in to the darkness calling to him.

When he found himself awakening several days later, he lay for a few moments, not knowing at first where he was. He looked down, seeing that his body was covered with bandages. A nurse came to check on him, looking at him quietly as she then moved to check his dressings. As she turned to a tray beside the bed, he tried to move, grimacing as pain shot through his body. The nurse heard him and turned around, smiling gently when she saw that he was awake. He strained again, trying to sit up.

"It would be better that you try not to move. You've been injured badly, Monsieur." He closed his eyes again. She moved over to him, looking at him quietly, a warm smile passing over her lips. "I'm glad you finally decided to join us. We weren't sure you would make it. In fact, a priest nearly performed the Last Rites when they found you on the field."

"What happened?"

"You were brought in with the last garrison sweeping the area for Germans. They didn't expect to find anyone alive."

He looked down, seeing restraints resting to the side of the bed. He frowned, staring at her quietly. The nurse shook her head, almost out of embarrassment.

"We had to put those on when you were brought in. By the time you reached the clearing station, you were coherent enough that you wouldn't let them operate on you."

Gascogne frowned, staring up into her face. "What did I say?"

Her voice dropped into a soothing tone as she looked at him quietly. "Some men see their wives and their children on the battlefield before they lose consciousness—particularly if they believe they are going to die."

The nurse could see he had once been handsome, his features strong, though with an air of refinement, as though he were one of the many aristocratic officers who had found himself leading infantry on the field. His records said that he was only forty-five, though like many of the other soldiers whom she had seen, there was little of his youth left. She peered upon him, seeing his battle scars, his face weathered by the elements and from the strain of leading men into battle. She could also feel his distance, seeing the faraway expression seeming permanently affixed in his hazel eyes, as though some part of him were still left on the field. She had seen the same odd stoicism on the faces of other officers who had been responsible for divisions of men who had died under their command, at no time revealing any of the emotion or guilt she would have expected. Instead their emotions were locked away, eating away at any possibility of peace as they retreated into the vast solitude of their minds.

She smiled again and touched his shoulder comfortingly, registering his discomfort in speaking. She turned away, moving behind him. Gascogne looked down at his body, seeing his entire right side covered with seeping bandages, despite having been newly changed. He grimaced, waiting out the moments of agony, as though just having seen the wounds reminded him to feel pain. He turned to find the nurse ready to administer his next shot of morphine. She watched him try to relax as she smoothed his dark hair from his forehead.

"Sleep now, Monsieur." She paused, the syringe ready as the needle pierced the skin on his arm, the thick, clear liquid entering his body. Immediately he closed his eyes. She removed the needle gently, and watched as he drifted off to sleep, marveling silently to herself that he was even alive.

"Soon you'll be away from this place," she said quietly. "And then perhaps you will have forgotten what you saw here."

He arrived in the small village near St. Girons weeks later, standing down from a lorry that had brought him several miles from the train station to town. As the lorry drove away, he paused, looking around him, seeing the mountains rising high in the distance which he had not seen since the beginning of the war. He could feel himself stiffen, despite his upbringing, not knowing now how to respond to those whom he had once known, and how they would respond when they saw him. He stood straight, surveying the territory which opened before him, once so familiar and now as though it had existed solely in some dream he had once several years before.

He wandered down the narrow street as the first signs of life stirred in the shops and through the windows of the houses he passed. He walked toward a small inn, seeing that the door was locked, no lights on inside. He approached the door and knocked on it softly, watching as an older woman appeared at the door.

"Oui, Monsieur—?"

She then looked at him more closely. She stopped, suddenly taking in her breath. Moments later she had covered him with her large body, squeezing him until he almost couldn't breathe, too overcome to remember any sense of decorum over a returning aristocrat. She let out a hearty laugh and pulled away from him, looking him over. She paused, her joy evident from the thankfulness in her eyes. "We weren't sure if you were alive or dead, Monsieur—but we hoped for the best…" She smiled, her eyes glistening. "It's good to have you home. Please come in."

Gascogne smiled slightly and walked inside as she closed the door firmly behind him. The old woman took the satchel from him, as she led him over to a chair, motioning for him to sit. She then moved over to the table, taking from it a glass and a decanter of red wine. She poured some and put it before him, watching as he took a healthy swig.

"There has been no one to run the vineyard—and we didn't know what your wishes were for it, so we let the few staff members go."

"No one has been to the house?"

"My husband goes once every few weeks to make sure everything is all right, though in its present conditions, it most likely would not be up to your standards, Monsieur. If I might suggest—you should stay here until you can decide whether or not it's livable."

He smiled. "Thank you, but I need to be home."

She nodded gently. "I'll have him take you. But first—let me get you something to eat. You will need something to warm you."

Gascogne watched as the older woman whisked herself away toward the kitchen, presumably to fix him something to eat. He looked quietly at the wine, placing the bottle back on the table after he poured more of the rich local vintage with his family's ancient name into his glass.

Later he rode silently beside the old woman's husband as he drove his cart slowly along the path several miles into the mountains. The old chateau stood on a high promontory a few miles from the village. It was in the same state as he had left it, the old stone structure run down, suffering the gradual deterioration from the many years it had stood against the elements. The old woman's husband watched him quietly as he saw the large stone structure rising from the path. Gascogne's expression was unwavering, as though its appearance were what he had expected.

They arrived several minutes later, and the innkeeper's husband helped him down from the cart. "You will be all right here, Monsieur?"

Gascogne smiled and nodded, reaching to shake the old man's hand in thanks for his kindness in bringing him back to his home. The old man reacted strangely, an odd expression moving over his face, as though unaccustomed to someone of Gascogne's station having taken such pains to offer him some degree of thanks. The old man then raised his hand briefly in a wave and drove back down the path toward the village.

Gascogne turned to the large stone residence looming before him, its rooms and halls showing nothing but its years of darkness, blackness seen only in the windows, which were shut tight. Gascogne stared at it silently, then moved forward, once again approaching the place he had not seen since he had left for the front.

Gascogne lit a fire, watching as the twigs caught flame. He could smell the dampness of the wood and stale smoke billowing in a narrow stream through the chimney. There were a few piles of wood left from when he had departed the chateau, having let most of the staff go, as he had not known whether or not he would return. Even now he preferred the silence and lack of disturbance. He closed his eyes, feeling the heat of the flames grow in the coolness of the night, light dancing across his face. The rest of the room was already shrouded in darkness, the sun having set.

Gascogne rose from before the fireplace, taking a bottle of wine with him as he opened the doors from his bedroom to walk outside. He stood against the stone railing of the terrace, looking across the hills which shone in the moonlight. The night was silent, the wind flowing gently against him. There were no lights, nothing but the moon's rays casting shadows against the treetops. All around he could feel a strange isolation, as there were no other signs of human life.

He opened the wine and began to drink, foregoing a glass and instead bringing the bottle directly to his lips. He could taste the wine's richness and its age, nothing like that which he had drunk on the front when men would sit under a darkened sky, dreaming of home, content to drown themselves and their sorrows before dawn. The wine requisitioned had been rich and pungently sweet, better than nothing, allowing the soldiers to drift off just long enough to restore themselves for the rigors of another day on the line.

He stared across the darkened landscape, seeing nothing of the vineyards that he knew had probably become overgrown or dormant since he had left. His family had owned it for centuries, one of the many families formerly of French aristocracy who had since lost their fortunes or who would, after enough time, fade into obscurity. Even now, there was no one left. No brothers or sisters, no other family, no one to continue their line or the tradition which they had somehow managed amidst all of the politics and revolution of several centuries to keep alive.

Gascogne stared out into the night, facing the silence alone. He could barely feel himself breathing, though he knew the blood continued to pump through his veins. Instead it was as though, like the rest of his ancestors who had died before him, he was one of the many spirits to inhabit the house, their portraits lining the walls in succession. He could feel them even now as though he were being watched, each of them whispering to him in the wind what he could expect from his isolation.

Gascogne slept in his room, the fire dying out beside his bed. The covers were dusty and smelling of dampness, holes eaten into the fabric from the insects coming to inhabit the house after their human predecessors had disappeared. Hearing a fluttering on the wall, he watched the moths attracted to the candle flame. He could only wonder how they knew how close to come before their wings caught fire, their bodies crisping from the heat. The image brought to his mind a sudden flash of human flesh burning, and he closed his eyes tightly.

Thunder sounded sharply from a storm moving over the mountain, flashes of lightning cast against the hills below, as the rain began, showering the room. He opened his eyes and rose, moving toward the doorway to close the doors. The mist from the storm hung heavily below, falling from the height of the chateau to cover the ground. The thunder continued, reverberating in a hollow echo against the mountains, shaking the ground underneath his feet. In his drowsiness, he stood, lost in an absent reverie, watching.

He had forgotten storms such as these, so unearthly that as a child he had climbed out of bed and over to the window, where he would curl himself into a ball, watching the storm as it moved across the foothills toward the village. He remembered that, moments later, someone would come in to check on him, most often one of his nurses, who would kneel beside him whispering into his ear, knowing that despite his fascination he would be afraid. "*Doucement, mon petit,*" she would say quietly, taking him into her arms. "*The Virgin will protect you.*" It was then that she would take him gently by the hand, leading him to his bed. She would cover him until he was nearly invisible underneath mountains of down, lying with him until he went back to sleep, safe in her arms. He remembered well the smell of her skin, the combination of lavender and strong soap, her hands rough from having worked as a girl in the vineyards. But even their roughness was comforting in those moments, as was the familiar sensation of her stroking his hair and telling him that everything would be all right, dreaming of the Virgin whom she had said would protect him. Within moments he felt himself sit on the floor and close his eyes, his thoughts racing as sleep began to claim him, flashes from his past, from the war and from his childhood coalescing into a stream of consciousness from which he did not want to awaken.

His eyes opened, however, a few hours later at dawn as a beam of light cast itself across his eyes from the sun which rose slowly over the eastern horizon. He could feel the air against his skin, cold and chilled from the dankness of the chateau. He rubbed his arms absently, as though to bring life back into his flesh which was stiff from having fallen asleep on the floor beside the open window.

He rose silently, for the first time in several years seeing the dawn which shone over the land that had once been his home. From the windows he could see the views of the countryside, the miles of landscape which now in the light still seemed uninhabited. He could hear nothing but the wind, the scent in the air of damp earth and stone.

He walked slowly through the house, surveying the rooms around him. Pieces of art hung on the walls, dusty and in a state of decay. What he had seen the night before, the once rich fabric which had adorned the furniture and had hung as drapes or in the tapestries on the walls had lain in shreds. No one had even entered the house to steal what might have been valuable. Instead all had been unceremoniously abandoned, as though even memory had been lost somewhere in the past.

He stood silently, realizing that nothing remained of his former life, or of the man he once was. Even before going off to war, he had known his life would end, having let the few remaining servants go after they had taken his orders to shut the windows or cover the furniture, closing everything within the stone structure as though preparing to leave everything behind. He had watched them leave, many of them men and women who had come from families who had worked this same land for generations. They had stared at him as though he were already a ghost, as though he were preparing for his own demise, staying a day longer before heading to the front.

He spent the next hour walking through the long hallways, entering corridors, examining the walls which were now stained, paint cracked and peeling from the stone. Floorboards creaked more than he had remembered, the wood rotting and infested with vermin. He had seen evidence of the rats and other rodents who had taken up residence once their human counterparts had gone.

Eventually he came before a large covered mirror in what had once been a richly-decorated parlor, its frame taking up nearly half the wall. He took the sheet from it, sliding it off. In the morning sunlight, the mirror reflected the light sharply into his eyes, though within moments, he saw his reflection. He was no longer the young man he had been. The handsome man with olive skin and preternaturally hued eyes had become worn and jaded. All around him in the room were covered pieces of art and furniture which would never again be used. As he looked at himself again in the mirror, he felt nothing. No pain, no regret, nothing but the same emotionlessness he had felt since he had been taken from the front lines.

He closed his eyes. It was then that in the light he saw her in his mind's eye, a woman's gray eyes shining. He was overtaken by the image from his memory, in his exhaustion his body growing heavy, and the image suddenly faded, leaving only a strange whisper in its wake. He could feel himself tremble, a cold chill moving through him.

Shaking himself free of the memory, he left the house and wandered through the gardens. Everything had overgrown from the recent years of neglect, hedges and trees unpruned, the fountain which had once been clear and filled with water from a nearby stream was now brackish, its surface covered with decaying leaves and algae. He looked around him, seeing the spindling black branches from dead brush and blackthorn. On the ground were tiles, now broken and stained, which he had remembered had been scrubbed every week by the servants so as to remain pristine, every other effort having been made to maintain the grounds with a care which had allowed the ancient chateau to breathe with new life. It, like all else, had now fallen to ruin, as though any life which might have remained was hidden, relegated to whatever dormancy to which it might surreptitiously cling instead of revealing itself to the harshness of the elements, no longer protected.

Before him was a grove of trees that still formed a canopy over an enclave made of stone. He headed toward it silently. He stopped, feeling the stone underneath his feet, seeing the statue before him, rising several feet from its platform. He looked up, staring into her eyes.

After a few moments, he could feel himself lowered to the ground, almost as though even his body could do nothing else but give way to the earth before her statue. Never before had he felt the emotions moving through him now, the pain which caused him to finally let go, even though he could not understand what it was that he felt. All he knew was that he had no protection left, and no one was there to watch him as he lost any last bit of resistance to the emotions which now flooded through him. He could feel himself trembling, his body curled into prostration before her, almost unable to breathe as he felt the sob in his throat, which after several moments he released, as though his whole body were mourning the last years, and what now brought him home.

Without looking, he could see her eyes in his mind, feeling the warmth which came from them, those same eyes which he had seen on the field, hearing the sound of a voice the softness of which he had never before heard as she had spoken to him. He could feel his eyes failing him as he tried to remember that the statue was made of stone, though for him, it may as well have been made of flesh and blood. For some reason he had been kept alive, something he had known without quite knowing why, though he could feel it with an intensity of emotion which had come, now, as he stood before the same figure whom he had been told would protect him as a child.

He paused, feeling his body shuddering, as though his soul were cracked open and exposed to the coldness of the air, the only warmth he could feel coming from his remembrance of those moments, feeling the presence of something he could not explain. There was nothing else within him left to question, as though in his exhaustion, he could feel amidst the pain within his body and soul, that perhaps she had waited for such a moment to reach him. The aristocrat from an ancient family was now feeling with the vulnerability of a child, bending at a mother's knee. His voice was barely audible as he whispered.

"Save me, Madame…for I am lost…"

Gascogne paused, looking out the window, again at

last light. In the years since, he knew that it had only been a matter of time before he would know his purpose. His eyes glistened, remembering. Despite everything, the months and years away, and even those hours in what had once been the place of his childhood, it had taken more than coming back to Gascony to remember the one thing which would allow him to feel at peace.

∞

Burke lay in his bed, asleep, his covers off, his body in a cold sweat as the storm rose around the hermitage outside, the wind beating against the stone. The wind seemed to affect him even as he slept, shuddering as though he could feel it against his skin. The sounds outside mingled with those in his dream as vivid images from the front flashed through his mind, those of his men, the haze of smoke and mustard gas, the sounds of men screaming, the sound of mortars and machine guns becoming so loud that it was like thunder in his ears, enough so that he didn't see the mortar coming, blasting through the sandbags of the parapet above the trench.

A company of British soldiers were at stand to at dawn in the rain, watching as a general, followed by two military attachés, each covered in rain gear, made an inspection, each of the men standing in several inches of mud. The general stopped before one of the men, a surly Cockney who was standing with another member of the infantry.

Burke watched them, not able to hear the commentary, seeing nothing but the long line of men grumbling, their bodies soaking in rain and mud, rats running through the trench to escape the downpour. The general moved forward, stopping on occasion to inspect his troops. He then paused, motioning behind one of the soldiers. The soldier stood aside, revealing a long, claw-like object sticking out of the dirt wall of the trench, the trench walls slowly disintegrating in the rain.

The general's face suddenly reddened with anger. Burke looked closely and realized that it was a gray-palled, decomposing arm and hand of a German soldier whose body, among others, had been inadvertently built into the trench wall. The general barked at one of the soldiers, who looked around for something to eradicate the offensive object, and, finding a shovel, hacked it unceremoniously from the trench wall.

Ypres. Troops from the Fifth Army crouched on the firing steps, the rain pouring. A young British soldier, perhaps not even twenty years old, huddled sobbing on the floor of the trench, hearing the screams of fellow soldiers falling around him from the parapet. His face was covered in blood, diluted by the rain until it fell in crimson streaks down his face. Shells of mustard gas fell, smoke wafting up around them as though in slow motion, several of the men beginning to choke, suffocated by the chemical reaction which burned in their lungs.

Men continued screaming at each other through the smoke of fire and the tear gas which landed several yards away, a few of them pulling masks over their heads while others fell, screaming in the midst of the fire. An officer screamed orders into the corps of soldiers, commanding them forward. Burke was down on the ground, his breath coming slowly, the sounds of battle fading into the background. The gas had already fallen, several of them not having donned their masks in time before they started to suffocate, their skin falling from flesh, disintegrating before his eyes. He turned, seeing a young solider slipping into the death throes, clawing at every exposed part of his body. Burke looked at him in horror, seeing a black cross emblazoned in ash across his forehead. Unable to put his mask on, his eyes burning from the gas, the boy clawed *viciously at his face, in his pain and horror, ripping his eyes from their sockets.*

In the background, all he could hear were screams coming from every direction, the dead falling back into the trench or on the field, smoke rising from the ground, coalescing with the mist until all he could see was a field of white. As he lost consciousness, he could hear the sound of something beating in the distance, a figure in silhouette approaching slowly across the field. He felt himself slipping away, his eyes focused forward. Her features soon became clear, her body tall and strong amidst the maelstrom. As everything faded to blackness, he saw her eyes, the crystalline grey depths looking quietly into his face, her hair down, flowing around her shoulders.

"Maeve…"

Burke awakened, shuddering, his body on fire, suddenly not knowing what was and was not a dream.

He ran through the forest, limbs whipping at his half-naked body, the wind bracing against him, battering him from every direction. The ominous sound of thunder exploded around him, following the flashes of light which streaked in jagged shards across the cimmerian sky, the Pyrenees rising in the distance.

Burke staggered through the brush, his chest heaving, his voice hoarse as he cried out into the maelstrom. His body was by now covered in streaks of earth and blood, lacerations cut into his skin. In the background, the wind moved among the trees, as it suddenly flowed through the leaves sounding eerily like whispers. He turned back, seeing the shadows and the path which was shrouded in blackness, as the storm continued around him. He could not tell where he had come from, disoriented by the storm and the images in his mind. Still in a daze, he raised his head to the sky. His voice came out in an agonized roar, unintelligible in the storm.

Gascogne grabbed several handfuls of kindling from the wood pile outside. The air was cold, as he shivered slightly, feeling the wind picking up again. He looked toward the horizon, seeing only the long, unbroken stretch of gray, unclouded sky. The storm had blown over for the moment, but he could still feel the dampness, as his breath condensed to a fine white mist in the coldness of the dawn.

He lowered his gaze, sensing the silence. There was a disturbance in the air, as though he could feel someone else close by. Not having ever felt it before while at the hermitage, he turned, looking briefly around him, scanning the ground. It was then that he saw a man's body just on the edge of the path, his face turned away, though the rest of him was face down in the cold dampness of the earth.

Gascogne walked over to him cautiously, seeing that he was unconscious. He noticed the tall, thickly muscled body covered in dark clothing, now in shreds. Long streaks of blood were carved into his skin, his breathing shallow.

Gascogne kneeled, reaching slowly to turn the man over. The man's face was rough, unshaven, his eyes closed, his rugged countenance blank of any sensation. Gascogne reached down, feeling his torso. The skin was tender by his ribs, visibly bruised with long welts from tree branches. Having seen his own soldiers suffering from the elements both before and after battle in the rain and cold, he recognized the effects of exposure. The man's skin was pale and unresponsive, as though his blood vessels were all too sluggishly returning blood to the surface of his skin when touched.

Gascogne leaned forward, pulling the man's arms in front of him, balancing the man's chest against the broadness of his back, then rising, pulling him upward so that he could carry him. Gascogne walked the several steps back to the hermitage, carrying Burke silently, then closed the door behind him.

Burke awakened, pain shooting through him as he felt the bed underneath where Gascogne had placed him. He closed his eyes, breathing in the stale air, the dampness from the storm and the smoke from his last fire mingling in the draft of the room.

Gascogne sat silently, watching the Irishman awaken. He placed more kindling on the fire as the wind howled sharply outside.

Burke opened his eyes again, attempting to move. He could feel the makeshift dressings Gascogne had placed against his chest to stop the bleeding.

"Don't move. Your body will need time to heal."

Burke heard the Frenchman's voice and looked down, seeing the bloodstained material, wincing as it moved against the tenderness of his flesh. He then turned back to Gascogne, watching as the Frenchman stood, moving over to look at him now that he was awake.

Burke frowned. "I don't suppose you have any whisky."

Gascogne smiled. He walked over to the table beside his chair, reaching for a bottle. He pulled out red wine, opening it as he began speaking again in his heavily-accented English. "Monasteries here don't have whisky. But they do have wine. It does the job."

He poured some for them both, handing one of the glasses to him, watching as Burke took a healthy swig. Burke remained silent, moving stiffly as he looked around the room. He noted the crucifix on the hearth, one which was similar to the one in his own hermitage before he had thrown it unceremoniously into the fire. Burke frowned, taking another swig as it washed roughly down his throat, not having drunk anything for several days.

"How long have I been here?"

"Two days. You had a fever which broke before dawn. Your ribs are broken, I'm not sure how many, but if you rest, and you keep them bound, you should be able to go back to your hermitage in a few days."

Gascogne returned to the fire and stood, stirring something in a pot placed over the flame. He ladled what looked like stew into a bowl and handed it to Burke. Gascogne then poured some for himself, sitting at the table beside the fire. "Eat. It looks like you haven't had anything since you came here."

Burke glanced at the stew and then placed the bowl on the table beside him.

"It's venison. Some of the monks catch roe deer in the forests and age the meat. You'll find that you can eat well here, if you care to. Everything you need you can find wild, outside of what the priory chooses to leave. Depending on the time of year, sometimes you have enough for quite a feast."

Gascogne paused, interrupted by the thunder outside, the rain continuing to fall in sheets against the thick lead glass of the windows. He then smiled slightly to himself.

"I remember nights like this when I was a boy. The woman who looked after me knew I would be afraid of the storm, so she would come into my room until I fell asleep. She used to work in the vineyards as a girl, so her hands were rough, but she always smelled of lavender. There were fields of lavender near us—ones that seemed to go on for miles. You could taste it in the grapes...in the wine. It seemed to dissolve into the air and come out like a perfume when it rained. Now when there is a storm, that is what I remember."

"You came from here."

Gascogne nodded. "This was once a part of my family's grounds. A family exists for hundreds of years and slowly fades into obscurity." He paused for a moment, shaking his head as though with amusement. "But then, that is the way of it. Everything has its time to live, and to die. A natural course for man, nature, and memory alike."

Gascogne poured more wine as Burke watched. In

the firelight Burke saw the scars marring the Frenchman's face, burns and small, deep gashes healed as thickened red skin across his neck which could only have been made by shrapnel.

"You were in the war."

Gascogne turned to him, seeing that he had noticed the marks on his face. "I was an officer in the Fourth French Army under Gouraud." He then paused. "Lascaux called me to the priory a few days ago to warn me about you. He doesn't understand your reasons for being here and thinks that perhaps you would take comfort in castigating the Church on Her own ground."

Burke snickered, taking another swig of wine. He then turned back to Gascogne, who had not stopped peering at him, though this time with a knowing expression on his face.

"It is something which is lost on them," Gascogne continued "...these men who have been here during the war. No one will ever know what we have seen except in the bars and brothels of Paris where one bargains away peace in order to escape. But there is no escape—nor is there the kind of peace one would think should exist. Perhaps not even here." Gascogne poured more wine. "Get some sleep. The more you rest the sooner you will be able to go back."

Burke had been awake for an hour, going in and out of consciousness. Several times he had awakened with his body shaking, only to have Gascogne come over to him, covering him with another of his own blankets. It was the least he could have done, Burke had known, seeing a veteran of the same, brutal war. Now he lay watching as Gascogne washed his clothing, which was covered in mud. In the firelight, he could see the torso of the Frenchman as he took off his own vestments, letting them dry by the fire as he blew into his hands trying to warm them. He then realized that Gascogne had gone back out into the storm for more firewood.

He watched, again seeing the Frenchman's scars, now realizing that one whole side of his body was covered in wounds which had healed, but most likely not without a great deal of pain. Gascogne heard him stirring and turned around.

Gascogne frowned. "It's good you are awake. You were talking in your sleep."

Burke nodded to Gascogne's wounds, to the jagged, deep gashes carved into his body. "Those are from shrapnel."

Gascogne nodded. "Yours will be worse. Those are from blackthorn." He laughed to himself and paused, sitting down before the fire. Gascogne breathed deeply, stoking the flames. "You said a woman's name while you were asleep." He then turned again, seeing the Celt's expression. Burke frowned, bowing his head. Gascogne nodded absently and then turned back toward the fire. "I had a wife and daughter. They both died during an epidemic which came through here while I was at the front. Before the war, I sent her off to her family near Bayonne. They kept her from coming home, thinking that she would escape from it there, but they both died within weeks. I didn't know they were dead until I received a letter from the priest."

"They buried them without telling you."

Gascogne nodded bitterly. "They blamed me for leaving her to be in the war." He paused for several moments, staring into the fire, as though remembering, a poignant expression flashing briefly across his eyes. "The war was not always popular here. Most of the people in this part of France are farmers. They watched their sons being slaughtered when the war was only supposed to have lasted a few months. The sons of the older families also died, even if, because of their position in society, they were commissioned as officers. When the pope suggested giving up Alsace and Lorraine to the Germans in return for peace, it seemed as though even he had chosen to be blind to the importance of those people whose sons had lost their lives. It took the archbishop in Paris to suggest singing 'The Marseillaise' as a prayer to undo the damage, to make us believe that the Church had not abandoned them. But even so there was more carnage than could be imagined, and not all was easily forgiven...or forgotten."

Gascogne looked at him curiously. "The woman whose name you said while you were unconscious...she was your wife?"

Burke frowned. Gascogne nodded, as though no words were even necessary. Burke watched as the Frenchman swigged Armagnac from a glass by his chair. He continued again, speaking gently. "I am not your confessor, Monsieur. Though I doubt either of us would be too pleasant to have in a confessional."

Burke then spoke. "She was a surgeon for the RAMC. We never married."

Gascogne breathed deeply, frowning. "What was her name?"

"Maeve."

Gascogne nodded. He then paused, the upcoming exposition the product of not having spoken to someone for some time. Even so, his manner was dignified, aristocratic, as though also used to being listened to when he chose to break what must have been an extended silence.

"I commanded a division of soldiers near Verdun before the Americans entered the war. The rail line leading south had been cut, and no reinforcements were to arrive for several days. The Germans had already taken Fort Douaumont. They launched phosgene and hit us with heavy artillery fire, flanking us on either side. They managed to kill several thousand men in a matter of hours. The men were disheartened, but they went on, as we were fighting on our own soil. For the Germans and Austro-Hungarians, as you know, it was an ancient exercise in conquest." He paused, looking at the fire. "I was different from other officers. I came from an old family, but my father had been a soldier, and I had been schooled in combat. But what I knew did little good that day. The field was covered in blood. Men were dying all around us when I moved forward from the command sap into the field. The shells they were firing had a mixture of shrapnel, explosives and gas. I had just moved forward when a shell hit a few feet away. I was thrown into a depression in the field. When I awakened, I was in a hospital behind the line. It turned out I had been on the field for two days. There is no reason I should have remained alive."

He shook his head, a powerful poignancy seeming to flood over him. "When I was a child, I used to visit a statue of the Virgin on our grounds, praying to go to war, to be a soldier like my father. At the time, I had wanted to make him proud. When I returned from the war, I went to Her again, asking why I had been kept alive. Who and what it was that had saved me. Here in Gascony, She is more than the Holy Mother. She and the land are holy, as is everything on it. The land which produces the wine which is the Blood of Christ. Before it had never meant anything to me, though in my own ways, I suppose I believed. I believed, perhaps, as a boy believes in fairy tales. It took the war for me to understand why I was here. The innocent wonder of a boy had gone. I was left instead with the doubts of a man who had lived through hell and the death of his family only to question why he was alive." He then looked at Burke, his voice unwavering.

"In those years of war, I had lost a part of my soul. It didn't matter to what God one prayed. Those over whom I commanded were Protestant, Jew, Catholic— each a man, each seeking to protect his soul from the hell he was forced to face. Without that salvation, he would not be able to remember who he was or what he was fighting for. In the end, the only thing which made sense was those whom he loved. That alone in the end is what transcended war—even religion—and the memories one suffered afterward."

Burke's jaw stiffened as he remained silent.

"Do not let pain make you forget, Monsieur. The woman you loved is with you always. For in loving her, you will always know what it means to know God. Perhaps that is what your Maeve would have wanted."

∞

...We are not who we once were, and the world we once knew is gone. Is this how others felt, once upon a time, in the passing of generations holding a torch aloft for empires which were drawing their last dying breaths? From the lies of the press and the indefatigable buffoonery of intellectuals and members of the peerage, lamenting the tide of civilization that has come crashing, full of words, but never themselves driven to action relegated to other men... Who are these men with endless words of victory—or bitter sorrow—when both offer cheap solace to those of us who, forever after, face wounds which will never heal? The smile of a man's own child and his arms about his neck when he returns home from the front will be torture enough, knowing how long he has been away. For who is the man who will put him to bed at night and kiss him on his forehead, but a shadow of the soul who once beheld him as an innocent, without word feeling the pride of one who once prayed his progeny would know a better world? For that man is not one we shall ever know again. He died on the field with his brethren, their souls wandering the fields of Verdun and Flanders while their battered bodies have returned home, changed forever by the horrors they have seen. No one but they will ever have the true ability to understand, though in certain moments, the only solace they may truly have, with their minds full of nightmares which keep them from sleep, will be the silence in certain moments which must take the place of peaceful dreams, and the hope that other generations will remember what has

been lost…

A young monk approached Lascaux in his study, carrying a tray with his supper. Before him Lascaux was studying a stack of yellowed papers, several more sitting on his desk. Beneath them the monk saw an envelope addressed from the archdiocese in Paris, the black ink written in the flourish of a bishop who had addressed the package to the abbot personally. The monk set the tray down, frowning as he looked at the abbot curiously.

"You've been in this room a long time, Father."

Lascaux paused, glancing at the monk for a moment before placing the article he had been reading on the desk. He raised it, showing the monk that it was from the trench newspaper *La Musette*, dated 1916.

"I've been reading since this morning. They wanted us to know the man whom they sent to us."

The monk frowned, looking again at the front page. He then saw Burke's name on one of the articles singled out among the rest. The young monk read a few lines, a strange feeling moving through him, as though the words had some effect he hadn't anticipated. He looked at the abbot again. "He is different than you thought."

"According to the bishop, our new retreatant had his uncensored accounts published in these papers…it seems even the priests at the front regarded him with a certain degree of reverence." Lascaux looked at another, picking it up gently, reading. "And it is true, I have never read anything like them. It seems there is more to the Irishman than even he would have us believe."

The monk paused, not understanding. Lascaux looked at the monk quietly, knowing such a young man had spent his life since childhood there, never having seen anything but the walls of the priory. What the men there understood, they understood in terms of doctrine and the tenets of service to a Church with which they had been reared, and to a God to whom the temporal world was but in service. And he had to believe such was the case even in war, even when so many had died. He turned to the young monk, seeing the innocence in the young man's eyes, knowing that had he not had such a haven where he could offer himself to the Church, he might have been one of those about whom Burke had written.

"It is said that the Irish are natural poets. But perhaps it is truly only in the real that a man finds his true poetry. Angels, demons— Heaven, Hell...they find their way every day into some man's soul. Since the beginning, the hell Burke has made is as real as any preached about from the pulpit. But it is only in facing that darkness that he and men like him will find Grace."

"So he has come to face his demons."

Lascaux shook his head. "No. He has come here to find what he has lost."

Burke had only been in the hermitage for a few days, time which had seemed to pass without thought, aided by a lack of consciousness from several bottles of wine and Armagnac which he had drunk while in the confines of Gascogne's hermitage.

Gascogne's condition had grown worse, as Burke could see from the pall in his expression, the Frenchman's skin growing more pale, his breathing continuing to be labored, though Gascogne had gone on to insist that he was fine. The Frenchman's expression itself over the last days had become that of a kind of resolved solemnity, as though he knew Burke's was the last human face he would ever see. Burke had remained silent, knowing that the Frenchman, in his reserve, would not have drawn attention to his condition or whatever thoughts might have gone through his mind. Instead he would allow all to be as it was, as it was a testament to his belief as much as it was to the experience they both had shared, even if it had been on different sections of the front. Within days, Burke had been well enough to leave, and when he had, no goodbyes were necessary, nor were any las words. Whatever understanding between them as men who had been through something unimaginable about which the rest of the world might never know, had been enough.

A few days later Burke discovered, on one of his rare trips to receive his provisions and not just the case of wine left for both men, that Gascogne had not touched what had been left for him. Burke walked along the path, feeling the coldness of the air against his face, the wind having picked up again as another storm came in. There was a strange glow in the distance, as the sun shone against the seamless backdrop of clouds in a muted crimson, which he knew meant that as the storms came in, the first snow of the season would begin to fall.

The hermitage looked cold and distant, uninhabited, no smoke from a fire, despite the chill which had come even more strongly in the last weeks. Outside, the sky was overcast, a dense layer of clouds having covered the sky so that the sun was completely hidden.

Burke walked to the door and knocked. Several moments passed, and he heard nothing. He knocked again, feeling the wind picking up, moving in from the sea in gusts which would have cut through anyone away from shelter. Burke waited, again feeling the temperature begin to drop. Still hearing nothing, he turned the handle on the door and walked inside.

He looked around, at first seeing no one. The room was cold, dark, the air stale and smelling of dankness, the windows closed tightly. He moved through the room silently, looking around him, frowning. It was as though no one had been there in days.

It was then that he saw the crumpled figure of a man, resting half-naked on the floor. Burke approached, kneeling and touching him gently. There was no response. Gascogne's skin was white, his body still. The last remnants of warmth were left, as Burke could see the faint trace of vapor moving into the air from his lips.

"Gascogne..."

Gascogne stirred slightly, opening his eyes. They were clouded, staring absently out into space. Burke took Gascogne in his arms, lifting him to his feet as he moved him to the bed. He placed him down gently, feeling bones jutting through the Frenchman's skin, his face sallow and drawn from a lack of sleep and nourishment. Burke bowed his head, his jaw tightening as he placed a blanket over Gascogne's body. Gascogne didn't move, though his chest continued to rise and fall, his breathing shallow.

Burke frowned, whispering harshly under his breath.

Burke made a fire, having brought in several pieces of wood from outside, snow covering several of the pieces of ash, which he knew would still burn. He knelt down, looking into a pot of stew, one which he had made while Gascogne was asleep.

Gascogne opened his eyes slowly as Burke came over to the bed. He glanced over to the fire, seeing the pot. He looked at Burke questioningly.

Burke chortled wryly. "You made me eat yours. Now you're going to eat mine."

Gascogne laughed weakly, reading Burke's concerned expression and knowing what he had been thinking. He hadn't seen himself for some time, but he knew his appearance was telling.

Burke sat next to the Frenchman, watching him eat. Gascogne had managed a few bites, placing the rest in its bowl on the table before sitting back against the pillows Burke had placed there for him. Gascogne stared at the Irishman quietly for several moments, looking into his face.

"The woman you loved...Maeve... She died during

the war."

Burke frowned, nodding silently.

"When I was with you last, while you were asleep, you were saying that you hadn't kept a promise to her. What was the promise you made to her?"

Burke paused, not sure he wanted to speak. He then turned, seeing the Frenchman's knowing expression, as though nothing might have surprised him.

"She asked me to say a prayer for her."

Gascogne smiled slightly to himself. "So that is why you came here."

Burke poured some wine, handing Gascogne a glass, who stared at it absently. He looked at Burke again, not paying attention to the Celt's attempt at diversion.

"There were men who used to pray to the Virgin before battle. They would sit before the first shot and say the rosary, praying for her intervention—that somehow they would be allowed to stay alive. Sometimes it seemed that their prayers were answered. Mons, the Virgin in Albert, and elsewhere." Gascogne looked out the window, watching the snow falling outside, the frost against the glass. He then continued, his voice weak, but unwavering. "I gave my life to Her because I knew that someday, when I had lived long enough, She would come for me. Perhaps then I would be allowed to be at peace." Gascogne frowned, certain thoughts moving through him which caused his expression to cloud. Burke looked at him quietly. Gascogne then smiled. Burke bowed his head again, feeling Gascogne looking at him kindly. "Some believe that suffering is the only way we come to know the Divine. That it is the only way we deserve absolution." Gascogne's gaze strengthened, as he looked pointedly into Burke's eyes. "But she is with you, always. She has been since the beginning. Even if you don't believe. And someday, when you have also lived long enough, and you have kept your promise, she will be waiting for you." Gascogne paused. "She knew you would keep your promise."

Burke frowned, bowing his head. Gascogne continued.

"Loving another, you are never the same. It is something which transcends everything else, including life and death itself." He paused, his eyes strong, warm, as he smiled, the power of his words evident, even to the Celt who sat before him. "The ones we love most, Burke, whether God or another human soul…they are the only reason we ever knew that we were truly alive."

The Frenchman was asleep when Burke finally closed his eyes, hearing the crackling of the fire beside him, and the sound of the wind outside. Burke sat still, his head cocked against the wall from having watched Gascogne for several hours. The wind had risen since, as Burke watched the limbs of the nearby trees swaying in the gales, their rhythm hypnotic until his eyes had begun to sting both from what he now knew and from a lack of sleep. Burke rose and walked over to Gascogne's body, kneeling before it. There was an uneasy silence. The Frenchman was still.

The world had suddenly seemed to grow black, as he listened to the howling of the wind outside, the ice cracking as the tree limbs moved in the frozen air. He then realized that for some time, the room had been calm, without sound, not even that of anyone's breath but his own. He then looked out the window, looking to the same point in the distance where the Frenchman had cast his gaze. He saw nothing but the coldness of the frosted glass and the snow that had begun to fall.

The world crumbled before him as he laid out Gascogne's body, placing it on his bed. When he was finished, he placed his hand on the Frenchman's chest, his own body trembling as though he were still feeling for a heartbeat, knowing that none existed. He paused for several moments, staring at a man who had been a fellow soldier, no one knowing what he had seen and who he had been, except for the journalist who had purposefully isolated himself. Burke shook as he reached down, holding one of the Frenchman's hands, which was still slightly warm. The other he placed across the Frenchman's chest.

"When they find you," he said quietly, "at least they'll know someone gave a damn."

Burke frowned, turning away. Beside the Frenchman on the table next to his bed, he saw Gascogne's few personal belongings, as though he had placed them there to remember the last several years of his life. As with most retreatants, they were allowed to keep little to remind them of their previous existence, nothing which would be able to come between them and whatever connection they sought with God. But apparently, Gascogne, like Burke, whether because of what had brought them there or some other reason, had managed to be exceptions. Burke reached over, taking from the table a book written in French. Underneath it lay an antique rosary, its beads made of deep garnet. Burke stared at it silently for several moments before touching the dark beads, feeling their smoothness underneath his fingers. An image of the soldier with whom he had ridden to the front before Maeve's death suddenly flashed through his mind. He then turned, looking again at Gascogne, a strange glow over him as the subtle rays of sunlight at dawn shone through the frost of the window. Burke bowed his head, a chill moving through him. He had seen death before, more than he or anyone else would ever have wanted, mostly in moments of horror and pain. Now he was seeing a man who had been where he had wanted to be at his death, having been a death which he knew must have come without fear. Despite himself, he could only wonder if the Virgin whom he had loved and had associated with his family had come for him in those last moments.

Burke looked again at Gascogne, staring down at his hands. His hands were scarred, his body tired and battered, much like his own. Suddenly Burke felt as though there were someone beside him. He breathed deeply, feeling a strange pain lodged in his chest, his skin going cold. Then, his hands shaking, Burke reached forward, placing the rosary gently in the Frenchman's hand. It was then that he heard Maeve's voice in his mind, recalling the gentle depth of her words the night before he had last seen her, and had left her at the camp. His body wracked with pain, he could feel himself continuing to shake, the words he had not said since he could remember, now finding themselves unconsciously on his lips. His jaw trembling, and his deep voice halting, he began to whisper.

> *Sé do Beatha Mhuire,*
> *Tá lán do ghrást, Tá an Tiarna leat.*
> *Is beannaithe thú idir mhná*
> *Agus is beannaithe toradh do bhrionne Íosa.*
> *A Naomh Mhuire mháthair Dé*
> *Ghúi orainn na bpeacaí*
> *Anois agus ar uair ár mbáis...*

Burke finished reciting the Rosary, seeing strengthening waves of light shining through the window, the warmth of it bathing Gascogne's body. He could feel himself break, the deep sob rising, unwanted, in his throat. He then felt his hands move up over his head, tears coming to his eyes, his strong body heaving, though the only thing that came out was the deep, regretful and unconsciously reverent prayer.

The wind came from over the mountains, whipping through trees. In the distance, lightning illuminated the dense front of clouds, the strong, cold air bracing against the hermitage.

He stared at her face in the photograph, as the wind howled outside. For a moment, he could feel the sense of isolation which had come since the Frenchman's death. For months he had thought of nothing but the satisfaction he had found, spurning the idea of another human presence, allowing himself the illusion that he could exist in his own world and not be affected by anything but the curse of his own regret. He had allowed his own isolation to surround him, seeping into him until he could convince himself that there was nothing left of him but the shell of what he had allowed to exist. It had been days before he had been able to recover, having been lost in some strange reverie.

Burke watched the snow falling against the window, ice crystals having formed on the panes. He walked over to the sill, feeling the coldness of the air against his skin, seeing the firelight in the window's reflection. Despite the cold, a chill moved across his skin, as though she were beside him.

He stood silently for several moments, his gaze losing focus as he found himself staring into the reflection, seeing the light of the flame of the fire behind him. He could almost imagine her, sitting before the fire, warming herself as winter raged outside. She was dressed as she had been during the war, in a man's shirt and worn brown breeches. He closed his eyes, seeing her turn, looking at him quietly, a wry smile on her face, her eyes warm and glistening as she rose, walking to him. He could feel her reaching around his waist, the warmth of her strong body against him, as she rested her head against his chest. She reached up, touching him gently, feeling the skin of his body, her own heart beating so that he could feel it against him. He did not want to open his eyes, fearing that she would not be there, that the only thing left would be the same, uneasy solitude and the sound of the wind, the same sound which for months had haunted him as he sat alone in the hermitage. Nothing else was important. Nothing else existed but the pain of not knowing whether or not she had forgiven him. That and the dreams which haunted his sleep.

But as he opened his eyes, he could still feel her. He could feel her presence as though she were there beside him, a physical body made of flesh and blood. It was then, despite any of the pain which still existed, he knew that some part of her indeed remained. And perhaps it was she who wanted him to be at peace.

He could hear her calling to him, the soft strength of her voice carried on the winds which for the last several days had battered the Pyrenees. His pen moved across the page, scratching against parchment. The only light which was visible was that of a candle resting beside him, illuminating only a portion of his face and his dazed, almost haunted expression, as though he were in another world.

He continued, bent over his desk, barely hearing the movement of the branches and the rustling of leaves as they moved across the nearly frozen ground, the oncoming maelstrom soon to follow. Outside the wind had continued its otherworldly sound, almost like those of whispers, fading in and out of the storm.

Burke looked down at the photograph, which he rested on the manuscript. He closed his eyes. He watched as she came before him, the same, gentle look in her expression, her strength shining in the gray depths of her eyes. He could feel her reaching forward to touch his face, her skin as warm as he had remembered it, the emotion again rising in him, overpowering him.

Burke reached forward, feeling his own fingers touching her face. He could now see her completely, feeling the warmth of her skin, feeling as real as anything he had ever felt. Tears suddenly burned in his eyes, relief moving through him as he finally allowed them to fall. He stared into her face, seeing the light which shone like a preternatural glow in her expression, her emotion enveloping him, as he could feel the words fall gently from his lips.

"Tá grá agam dhuit..." he said quietly. "Maeve...I love you."

The sun was streaming over the landscape, the snow having fallen without ceasing for several days. The young monks approached the hermitage slowly, not wanting to disturb anyone lest Gascogne be asleep inside. Seeing no one, nor any sign of life, they walked to the door.

The door opened slowly, with one of the monks walking inside. They saw nothing for several moments when each finally braved entrance, only the state of the hermitage, a layer of dust covering everything in sight. One of the monks stepped further, cautiously looking around. He then turned, seeing a figure unmoving in his bed.

The monk walked to him, pulling the cover away, seeing the body of the Frenchman, his hands over his chest, holding his rosary, his eyes closed. The monk bowed his head, saying a silent prayer.

"Monsieur…"

Lascaux turned, seeing a monk who had stepped inside the doorway, motioning to one of the other men outside. Lascaux frowned, rising slowly, by the expression on the young monk's face, not wanting to ask any questions.

Lascaux walked slowly through Gascogne's hermitage, the first light of morning streaming through the lead glass windows, his breath still visible in the cold. He could feel his jaw tense as he stared at Gascogne's unmoving figure on the bed.

Lascaux stood with several monks before the hermitage, Gascogne's body still inside. Lascaux paused, feeling the wind as he stared at the structure, then turned, seeing the monk who held a torch aloft, waiting for Lascaux's signal. Lascaux nodded, watching the monk walk forward, setting the structure aflame. The others looked on, a few of them turning in morbid curiosity, but remaining silent.

Lascaux watched for a few more moments, seeing the stone begin to blacken, the wood inside lighting, despite the cold and the snow on the ground. Within several more seconds, everything inside began to smolder, and Lascaux knew that soon enough, nothing else would exist.

Lascaux raised his hand marking the sign of the cross as he whispered to himself the Last Rites, watched the structure dissolving into blackness.

Another monk approached, as Lascaux turned. "The Irishman."

Lascaux looked at him quietly.

"He has gone."

Lascaux nodded silently. "Was there anything left in the hermitage?"

The monk nodded. "Something he left for you."

The monk handed him a note, and with it, a sheaf of paper, on which was the Irishman's handwriting, over a hundred pages of his small, even cursive.

Lascaux read the first few lines and bowed his head. His own words came to him from a time before, resonating now with greater force.

"So he has come to face his demons."

"No. He has come here to find what he has lost."

EPILOGUE
LONDON 1933

HAVE you forgotten yet?...
For the world's events have rumbled on since those gagged
days,
Like traffic checked while at the crossing of city-ways:
And the haunted gap in your mind has filled with thoughts
that flow
Like clouds in the lit heaven of life; and you're a man
reprieved to go,
Taking your peaceful share of Time, with joy to spare.
But the past is just the same--and War's a bloody game...
Have you forgotten yet?...
Look down, and swear by the slain of the War that you'll
never forget.

Do you remember the dark months you held the sector at
Mametz—

The nights you watched and wired and dug and piled sandbags
on parapets?
Do you remember the rats; and the stench
Of corpses rotting in front of the front-line trench--
And dawn coming, dirty-white, and chill with a hopeless rain?
Do you ever stop and ask, 'Is it all going to happen again?'
Do you remember that hour of din before the attack—
And the anger, the blind compassion that seized and shook
you then
As you peered at the doomed and haggard faces of your men?
Do you remember the stretcher-cases lurching back
With dying eyes and lolling heads--those ashen-grey
Masks of the lads who once were keen and kind and gay?
Have you forgotten yet?...
Look up, and swear by the green of the spring that you'll
never forget.

-- "Aftermath," Siegfried Sassoon, March 1919

The wind was howling outside the townhouse window as Harrold sat silently, the manuscript lying beside him. It had been hours since he had seen Peter in the Cambridge Club, though it seemed longer, as though years which had been forever imprisoned in his mind had suddenly been allowed to play themselves out, moment by moment, as he had read Burke's words. He could feel the silence of the house, the strangeness of it, the draft of the room moving against his skin, and the words Burke had written haunting him. For hours he had sat reading, in certain moments not having been able to withstand the emotions which continued to bombard him, as though they would no longer remain locked safely in the past. The abbot had taken whatever efforts he could to find him, which had extended beyond his own death. It had only been his successor, charged with the task, who had found him. And it was now all the more poignant as the world was starting again to be embroiled in conflict from which, he thought bitterly, it seemed that war, if not now, would again find a way to come. It had only made his memories all the more powerful now with the Celt's words in his hand.

Harrold paused, turning to look at the wall. Beside the fireplace was an antique box where he had placed the few relics he had kept from the front. He had not opened it since the day he had seen Burke all of those years before, before the surly Irishman had left for France. He remembered locking those last remembrances away, opening a bottle of expensive whisky and drinking until felt himself slipping safely into oblivion. In the years since, there had been nothing else to remind him of them except their photographs, which all he had been able to see without feeling the immense power of memories which he had believed were better left in the past.

He rose unsteadily from the chair, walking slowly over to the shelf. He paused for a moment, then took the box from its place. He could feel the heaviness of it in his hands, the lid sliding open, his body trembling as he looked inside. There he saw a copy of *An Choiméide Dhiaga*, Burke's, and Maeve's rosary.

He opened the book, the leather binding cracked and worn. He turned to the page Burke had once marked, in a book about heaven and hell written hundreds of years before, translated into Irish. He felt his chest become heavy as he read the title, and the passage which Burke had translated which he now knew by heart, having read it silently in his chair only hours before.

Harrold paused, his head bowed to his chest, feeling the emotion move through him. For years he had not allowed himself to remember them or remember anything of who he once had been. For those years during the war were the years of his life, he realized, when he had most been himself. No matter who they had been before the war, and who either man had become afterward, the only thing which had mattered was who they had been in those weeks. For Harrold would never know again the same depths which had come from the two people whom he remembered in his life above all else, the both of them having been, even now, and regardless of what he may or may not have chosen to remember over the years since the war, the only ones who had known most who he was. And he knew, after reading the Celt's words, what they both would have wanted.

He had never been to the place where he now stood, steep black cliffs, the sound of the waves, the mist rising from the water, making little visible against the horizon. Harrold stood silently, staring into the distance. Within moments, the sun would set, and he would be forced to leave this place, perhaps never to return to it again. He stared out at the horizon, listening to the waves breaking against the cliffs. It was then that he looked down at what he held in his hand. The gleaming beads of the antique rosary shone in the last rays of sunlight. The reflection cast against his hand, the combination of reflection and shadow which reminded him of them both— the discernment, the strange, eternal beauty of a man and woman whom he could feel as though they were standing beside him, staring out into the same distance. Feeling their presence, he cast the rosary into the sea.

Harrold bowed his head, closing his eyes. He felt a sense of peace, knowing that they both were somewhere unseen, somewhere beyond, in another world. And more importantly, if he believed what he felt in those moments staring out to the sea, that when his time came, they would be waiting for him.

ACKNOWLEDGEMENTS

This book would not have been possible without research done from sources truly invaluable, both in terms of chronology and the details necessary for the story itself. The most important of these in terms of research materials were *World War I*, by S.L.A. Marshall (Copyright ©1964, Mariner Books/Houghton Mifflin Company), as its truly extensive detail and expertise in terms of the nature of the war were only matched by the humanity of the author's prose, making at times pointed commentary about the battles and the commanders themselves. Other works included *World War I: A Visual Encyclopedia* (Copyright ©2002, PLC Ltd.); *They Shall Not Grow Old: Irish Soldiers and the Great War*, Myles Dungan (Copyright © 1997, Four Courts Press); *The War in the Trenches*, Alan Lloyd (Copyright © 1976, David McKay Company, Inc.); *The Killing Ground: The British Army, the Western Front & The Emergence of Modern Warfare 1900-1918*, Tim Travers (Copyright ©1990, Unwin Hyman, Ltd.); *The Great War in Africa 1914-1918*, Byron Farwell (Copyright © 1986, W.W. Norton & Company, N.Y.) and *Into the Breach: American Women Overseas in World War I*, Dorothy and Carl J. Schneider (Copyright © 1991, Viking, N.Y.). Also of incredible assistance were sources on the Web, most notably from the Great War Society (http://www.worldwar1.com).

First, in personal thanks, to the late Joe Kruzel, who asked me to come back to this path before his death in 1995, not realizing that both literature and war would have a profound effect on my life—including in ways merging the two areas of importance.

To Jon H., for having read various drafts of this and the script when I first wrote them, while taking care of my father, letting me know how it read and how you felt reading it. Both of us having veteran fathers and family, I knew you understood why I had to write this.

G., thank you for giving me a personal view of the British military and getting opinions from your old instructors at Sandhurst, including the one luminary whose reaction I will always feel, deeply and thankfully.

Krista Minteer-Baysal, for going over this with your keen eye—it made a profound difference.

To a truly treasured friend and fellow lover of both books and single malt Scotch, Michael Dalling, being British and a former correspondent first told me how much the story meant to him.

Warmest thanks go, too, to my other close friends and family, all of whom watched me work on both the book and the accompanying script over the last many years in varying incarnations and offered unending support, particularly under the circumstances and time during which I had to write them. Indeed, not wanting to forget anyone, I could not have done this without any of you. But special thanks go, always, to Pamela I. Theodotou (and of course you, Tom Starker), who were there during some of my toughest moments...I will never forget your love and kindness when I needed it the most. (You were also quite good at giving me a good, swift kick in the ass when I most needed it.)

Saru, because I know you "get it"...and thank you for that.

Last but not least, this book was also written in memory of my beloved mother and my late father, a veteran and the man whom our family considered our own Atticus Finch, whom I was proud to be with during the last years of his life. Since I was a child, they believed that one day I'd write something like this, and their love, support, and confidence--I will remember always.

May all of us, too, remember the veterans of this war, among those of other wars, past and present, I hope will never be forgotten, as their courage and sacrifice are such that we should always offer thanks in their remembrance. For war itself will always have a profound effect upon both the world itself and humanity in the most profound of ways as long as it shall continue to exist.

K.J.W.

Made in the USA
Columbia, SC
28 November 2022

72187172R00098